SECRET SEVE
THREE CHEER
SECRET SE

D0832080

Enid Blyton

THE
SECRET
SEVEN

SECRET SEVEN WIN THROUGH

THREE CHEERS, SECRET SEVEN

SECRET SEVEN MYSTERY

*Hodder
Children's
Books*

a division of Hodder Headline Limited

This collection published in 2005
by Hodder Children's Books
For sale in the Indian Sub-continent only.

Secret Seven Win Through first published in Great Britain in 1955
Three Cheers, Secret Seven first published in Great Britain in 1956
Secret Seven Mystery first published in Great Britain in 1957

For further information on Enid Blyton please contact
www.blyton.com

6 8 10 9 7

A Catalogue record for this book is available from the
British Library.

ISBN 0 340 91091 7

Typeset by Hewer Text Ltd, Edinburgh
Printed and bound in India by
Gopsons Papers Ltd., Noida

Hodder Children's Books
a division of Hodder Headline Limited
338 Euston Road
London NW1 3BH

SECRET SEVEN WIN THROUGH

[1]

The holidays begin

'Easter holidays at last!' said Peter. 'I thought they were never coming. Didn't you, Janet?'

'Yes. It was a dreadfully long term,' said Janet. 'We've broken up now though, thank goodness. Don't you love the first day of the hols, Peter?'

'You bet! I get a lovely *free* sort of feeling,' said Peter, 'and the hols seem to stretch out in front of me for ages and ages. Let's have some fun, Janet!'

'Yes, let's! April's a lovely month – it's warm, and sunny too, and Mummy will let us off on picnics any day we like,' said Janet. 'Scamper, do you hear that? Picnics, I said – and that means rabbit-hunting for you, and long, long walks.'

'Woof!' said Scamper at once, his tail thumping on the floor, and his eyes bright.

'You're the best and finest golden spaniel in the whole world!' said Janet, stroking his silky head. 'And I do so love your long, droopy ears, Scamper. You like it when we have holidays, don't you?'

'Woof!' said Scamper again, and thump-thump-thump went his tail.

'I vote we have a meeting of the Secret Seven as soon as we can,' said Peter. 'To-morrow, if possible. Picnics and things are much more fun if we all go together.'

'Yes. Let's have a meeting,' said Janet. 'What with exams and one thing and an-other all the Secret Seven have forgotten about the Society. I haven't thought a word about it for at least three weeks. Gosh – what's the password?'

'Oh, Janet – you haven't forgotten that *surely*?' said Peter.

'You tell me,' said Janet, but Peter

wouldn't. 'You don't know it yourself!' said Janet. 'I bet you don't!'

'Don't be silly,' said Peter. 'You'll have to remember it by tomorrow, if we have a meeting! Where's your badge? I expect you've lost that.'

'I have *not*,' said Janet. 'But I bet some of the others will have lost theirs. Somebody always does when we don't have a meeting for some time.'

'Better write out short notes to the other five,' said Peter, 'and tell them to come along tomorrow. Got some notepaper, Janet?'

'Yes, I have. But I don't feel a bit like sitting down and writing the first day of the hols,' said Janet. 'You can jolly well help to write them.'

'No. I'll bike round to all the others and deliver the notes for you,' said Peter.

'Now it's *you* who are silly,' said Janet. 'If you're going to everyone's house, why not *tell* them about the meeting. All this note-writing! You just *tell* them.'

'All right. It just seems more *official* if we send out notes for a meeting, that's all,' said Peter. 'What time shall we have it?'

'Oh, half-past ten, I should think,' said Janet. 'And just warn Jack that he's not to let his horrid sister Susie know, or she'll come banging at the door, shouting out some silly password at the top of her voice.'

'Yes. I'll tell him,' said Peter. 'The worst of it is, Susie is so jolly sharp. She always seems to smell out anything to do with the Secret Seven.'

'She would be a better person to have *in* a club than out of it,' said Janet. 'But we'll never, never let her into ours.'

'Never,' said Peter. 'Anyway, we can't be more than seven, or we wouldn't be the Secret Seven.'

'Woof!' said Scamper.

'He says he belongs, even if we're seven

and he makes the eighth!' said Janet. 'You're just a hanger-on, Scamper, but we simply couldn't do without you.'

'Well, I'm going to get my bike,' said Peter, getting up. 'I'll go round and tell all the others. See you later, Janet. Coming, Scamper?'

Off he went, and was soon cycling to one house after another. He went to Colin first, who was delighted to hear the news.

'Good!' he said. 'Half-past ten? Right, I'll be there. I say – whatever's the password, Peter?'

'You've got all day to think of it!' said Peter, with a grin, and rode off to Jack's. Jack was in the garden, mending a puncture in the back wheel of his bicycle. He was very pleased to see Peter.

'Meeting of the Secret Seven tomorrow morning in the shed at the bottom of our garden,' said Peter. 'I hope you've got your badge, and that your awful sister Susie hasn't found it and taken it.'

'I've got it on,' said Jack, with a grin. 'And I wear it on my pyjamas at night, so it's always safe. I say, Peter – what's the password?'

'*I* can tell you!' said a voice from up a near-by tree. The boys looked up to see Susie's laughing face looking down at them.

'You don't know it!' said Jack fiercely.

'I do, I do!' said the annoying Susie. 'But I shan't tell you, and you won't be allowed in at the meeting. What a joke!'

Peter rode off to the rest of the Seven. That Susie! She really was the most AGGRAVATING girl in the whole world!

[2]

A dreadful blow

Next morning Peter and Janet began preparing for the meeting. Meetings weren't proper meetings, somehow, unless there was plenty to eat and drink while they talked. Their mother was always generous in giving cakes or biscuits and lemonade, and the two children went to find her.

'Hallo,' she said, looking up from chopping parsley on a board. 'What are you two after now?'

'We're going to have a Secret Seven meeting,' explained Peter, 'and we wanted something to eat and drink.'

'Well now, let me see – you can have that tin of ginger biscuits – they've gone soft,' said Mummy smiling. 'And you can make yourselves some real lemonade – there are plenty of lemons and sugar in the larder.'

'Ooh, good!' said Janet. 'I'll do that. I'll make it with hot water, and let it go cool. Anything else we can have?'

'Jam-tarts,' said Mummy, chopping away hard at the parsley. 'Only four though, I'm afraid. That's all that were left from supper last night.'

'Four – well, we'll halve them,' said Peter. 'There'll be one half over, so . . .'

'Woof! woof!' said Scamper, at once. The children laughed.

'All right, you shall have the half left over,' said Peter. 'You never miss a word of what we say, do you, Scamper?'

Janet made the lemonade, and Peter got the tin of biscuits and found the tarts. He cut them carefully into exact halves and put them on a plate.

'Come on, Janet,' he said. 'It's nearly half-past ten.'

'Peter, please do tell me the password!' said Janet. 'I'm very, very sorry I've forgotten it.'

'No. I shan't tell you,' said Peter. 'You'll have to be in the shed, anyhow, and you can jolly well listen to the others coming along and saying the password, and feel ashamed of yourself!'

'You're mean!' said Janet. 'Isn't he mean, Scamper?'

Scamper didn't answer. 'There,' said Peter, 'he won't say I'm mean. He never will. Do come on, Janet. I'm not going to wait a minute longer.'

Janet was ready. She put the jug of lemonade and seven unbreakable mugs on an old tray and followed Peter out of the kitchen. 'Thanks, Mummy!' she said, as she went carefully down the steps outside the kitchen door.

Peter was ahead of her. He went along the path that wound between the bushes right down to the bottom of the garden, where the old shed stood that they used for their meetings. On the door was always pinned the sign 'SS'. How many, many times the Secret Seven had met there and made exciting plans!

Janet followed a little way behind, carrying her tray carefully. She suddenly heard Peter give a startled shout, and almost dropped the tray she held.

'What's the matter?' she called and tried to hurry. She came in sight of the shed – and stared in horror.

The door was wide open, and so were the windows. Everything had been turned out of the shed! There were boxes and cushions and sacks, all strewn on the ground in untidy heaps! Whatever had happened?

Janet put her tray down, afraid that she might drop it in her dismay. She looked at Peter in despair.

'Who's done this? Just as we were going to have a meeting too! It's too bad.'

Peter looked into the shed. It was quite empty, except for the shelves round the sides. He was puzzled.

'Janet – it couldn't be Susie, could it?' he said. 'I mean, this is an awful thing to do, throw everything out of our shed. I don't think even Susie would do that.'

'She might,' said Janet, almost in tears. 'Oh, our lovely meeting-place!'

'Here come the others,' said Peter, as Pamela and Barbara appeared down the path together. They stared in amazement at the untidy mess on the ground.

'What's happened?' said Barbara. 'Are we too early?'

'No. We've only *just* seen all this ourselves,' said Peter. 'Hallo – here's Jack. Jack, look here.'

'Gosh!' said Jack. 'Who's done this? It can't be Susie. She's been with me all morning till I left just now.'

Colin and George came up just then, and

the Seven looked ruefully at the boxes and cushions thrown out so untidily. 'We'd better put them back,' said Janet. 'And we'll find out who's done all this to our secret meeting-place.'

They began to put everything back, and then they heard footsteps coming along down the path. Who was it? Peter looked to see.

It was the gardener, carrying a strong broom over his shoulder, a pail of water in his hand, and some cloths hanging on the side of the pail. He stared at the Seven in annoyance.

'Hey, you! What are you doing? I've only just thrown all that rubbish out!'

'But why?' demanded Peter, indignantly. 'This shed is our meeting-place, and this isn't rubbish. We use it.'

'Oh, well, I don't know anything about that,' said the gardener. 'All I know is that your father told me to clear out this place,

burn all the rubbish, and do a spot of paint-
ing. He said it was going to rack and ruin,
and he wanted it cleaned up.'

'I see,' said Peter, his heart sinking. If his
father had planned this, there was nothing to
be done. He turned to the others. 'Come on,
let's find somewhere to talk,' he said. 'We
can't meet in our shed for a while, that's
certain. How annoying!'

'Never mind! We'll think of somewhere
just as good,' said Colin. But nobody agreed
with him. They thought the shed was the
finest place in the world for Secret Seven
meetings!

The Seven, followed by Scamper with his
tail well down, went slowly up the garden
path. Somehow it seemed dreadful not to
have their usual meeting-place.

'We'll go to the summer-house,' said Peter.
'Oh, look, there's Mummy, Janet. We'll ask
her about the shed.'

'Mummy!' called Janet. 'Why didn't you

tell us the shed was going to be cleaned and painted – our own shed, I mean, where we meet? I do think *somebody* might have told us.'

'Oh dear, I quite forgot to tell you that Daddy wanted it cleaned and mended,' said her mother. 'It was almost falling to bits here and there, you know. But you can have it for a meeting-place again when it's finished. It will look nice and bright and clean then.'

'But we like it old and dark and untidy,' said Peter mournfully. 'And I do think it's a pity to have it done in the holidays, Mummy, just when we want to use it.'

'Yes, I agree, it is a pity,' said Mummy, looking very sorry. 'I would have stopped it if I'd known that it was to be done just now. Well – you'll have to find another meeting-place. What about the attic?'

'Oh no,' said Janet. 'It's no fun meeting in a *house*, with other people in near-by rooms. We want a secret, lonely place, we do really.'

'Yes . . . I suppose you do,' said her mother. 'Well, I can't suggest one, I'm afraid. Go to the summer-house just for now.'

'We were going to,' said Peter, still very doleful. Soon they were all squashed into the little old summer-house. They didn't much like it, because it was rather earwiggy.

They began to eat the ginger biscuits. 'Rather soft, I'm afraid,' said Janet.

'Oh, I like them soft and squidgy,' said Pam. 'I hate them when you have to bite so hard they splinter in your mouth. Hey, this is good lemonade! Did your mother make it, Janet?'

'No. I made it myself,' said Janet proudly. 'Peter, hadn't we better talk about where to have a new meeting-place?'

'Yes,' said Peter. 'And I vote that we all of us have a good hunt round to find somewhere, some absolutely secret place that even Jack's sister Susie won't find. It mustn't be too far away. I'll give you today to find one.

Meet here this evening, in this summer-house again, at six o'clock.'

'Right,' said Colin. 'I think I know of one already.'

'Well, don't tell us now,' said Peter. 'We'll each give in our ideas this evening and put it to the vote to see which is the best. We must do these things properly.'

'Yes,' said everyone, and took a drink of Janet's lemonade.

'What about the password?' said Jack. 'We were all so upset about the shed that we never even gave the password.'

'We've all got our badges on,' said Pamela. 'I had an awful hunt for mine. I put it in such a safe place that it was almost too safe for me to find!'

'Where was it?' asked George.

'I buried it in the pot of maidenhair fern my mother has in the drawing-room,' said Pam, with a giggle. 'And then forgot about it. It took me ages to remember it.'

'I thought it looked a bit grubby,' said Peter. 'I think that's a silly place.'

'Oh, I wrapped it in paper,' said Pam. 'But I forgot that the fern gets watered twice a week – so, of course, the paper soaked off and made my badge messy.'

'It's a good thing it didn't put out roots and grow!' said Peter. Everyone laughed.

'Peter, could we have a new password?' said Jack. 'Susie knows our last one. I'm most dreadfully sorry, and I don't know how she knew it, unless she hung round our last meeting and heard it.'

'All right. We'll choose a new one,' said Peter. 'It's time we did, anyway. I must say that your sister Susie is getting worse and worse, Jack. I hope she's nowhere about just now.'

Jack got up and went out of the summer-house. 'Nobody's anywhere near,' he said. 'Quick – what's the new password?'

'Easter-egg,' said Peter. 'That's easy to remember, because it's the Easter holidays.'

'Easter-egg,' repeated everyone, in low voices. Pam took out a notebook and began to write it down.

'Don't *you* write it down, Jack!' said Janet, 'or Susie will find it. I wonder how she knew our last password?'

'Well, she called out, "Your password is Sugar-mouse" just as I was leaving,' said Jack. 'And I don't mind owning up now that I was really glad to hear it, because I'd forgotten it completely.'

'Sugar-mouse!' said Peter, in astonishment. 'It was nothing of the sort. Susie just made that up because she knew you'd forgotten it. She hoped you would rap on the door of the shed and yell out "Sugar-mouse" and make a fool of yourself.'

Jack went red. 'What was the password then?' he said. 'Janet, you tell me. Peter won't.'

Janet went red too. '*I've* forgotten it as well,' she said.

Pam blushed as red as Janet, so Peter knew she had forgotten too! He rapped on the summer-house table.

'The last password was a very simple one,' he said. 'It was "Thursday". Just that, "Thursday".'

'Gosh, so it was,' said Barbara. 'I just couldn't remember if it was "Thursday" or "Friday".'

'*I* thought it was "Sunday",' said Colin, with a laugh. 'It was a silly password to choose, Peter, too easy to muddle up with the other days of the week. "Easter-egg" is much better.'

'Well, let's hope that Barbara and Colin don't mix it up with "Christmas present" or "Birthday gift"!' said Peter. 'Now – we've eaten everything, and Scamper's had his half-tart, and we've drunk all the lemonade – what about separating and hunting for a new meeting-place?'

'Right,' said everyone and got up. They all

went off up the path to the front gate, and most of them were murmuring two words to themselves as they went.

'Easter-egg! Easter-egg! I must remember Easter-egg!'

[3]

Plenty of ideas

At six o'clock that evening there was a continual noise of footsteps up the path to the little summer-house. Janet, Peter, and Scamper were inside, waiting.

'Easter-egg,' said Jack, walking inside. There was no door, for the summer-house was three-sided, with its fourth side open to the garden.

'Easter-egg,' said Barbara, walking in, too.

'Where's your badge?' asked Peter sharply.

'Oh – I've got it, it's all right,' said Barbara, feeling in her pocket. 'I don't know why I forgot to pin it on.' She pinned it on carefully and sat down.

The other three came along, each solemnly giving the password.

'For once nobody *yelled* it out,' said Peter. He took a notebook out of his pocket, and licked his pencil. 'Now then. I want your reports on any likely places to meet secretly. Colin, you begin.'

'Well, there's a fine big tree at the bottom of our garden,' began Colin hopefully. 'It's a great chestnut, and . . .'

'No good, I'm afraid,' said Peter, 'but I'll put it down. It would hardly be a secret meeting-place! Everyone would see us going down the garden to it, and people passing the wall nearby would hear us up there. Barbara, what's *your* idea?'

'Oh, it's a silly one,' said Barbara. 'There's an old hut in a field nearby our house, and . . .'

'I know it,' said Peter, scribbling in his notebook. 'Not a bad idea, Barbara. You, Pam?'

'I simply haven't any idea at all,' said Pam. 'I've thought and thought, but it's no use.'

'*Not* very helpful,' said Peter, putting a cross against Pam's name in his notebook. 'You, George?'

'Well, there's an empty caravan in a field not far from here,' said George. 'I know who owns it – it's a friend of my father's. I think I could get permission for us to use it.'

This sounded exciting. Everyone looked admiringly at George, who seemed quite pleased with himself.

'You, Jack?' said Peter. 'And don't suggest anywhere near *your* house, because of Susie.'

'I'm not going to,' said Jack. 'I'm not quite so silly as that. I've chosen somewhere a long way away, down by the river. It's an old boathouse that nobody ever uses.'

This sounded exciting too. Peter wrote it down solemnly. 'Now we've heard everyone's idea except mine and Janet's. We went out hunting together, and Scamper came too – and we've all got the same idea.'

'What?' asked everyone.

'Well, it's a cave in the quarry near the field where we grow potatoes,' said Peter. 'So it's on my father's farm, and not very far. It's absolutely lonely and secret, and goes back into the hill behind the quarry. Scamper found it, actually.'

'That sounds good – a secret cave,' said Pam.

'Well, we'll now put all our ideas to the vote,' said Peter, and handed round slips of paper. 'Please write down on these papers what ideas you like best – but nobody must vote for their own idea, of course. I'll just go shortly over them again:

'Colin suggests a tree, but it's not a very *secret* place. Barbara suggested that old hut in the field near her house – but the roof's almost off and the rain would come in. Pam has no ideas. George suggests the caravan owned by his father's friend, a very good idea, but I don't honestly think we'd be allowed to use it because it's still furnished. I'd be afraid of breaking something.'

Peter paused for breath. 'Jack suggested the old boathouse by the river. Fine – but isn't it rather far away for a meeting-place? It's at least a mile away. And you know what Janet and I suggest – the cave. But that isn't a really comfortable place. There you are – please vote on your papers, fold them in half, and give them to me.'

Everyone solemnly wrote something on their papers, then handed them to Peter. He opened them and read them. When he looked up, his eyes were shining with pleasure.

'Er – well – it's very funny, but everyone except me and Janet have voted for the cave. We couldn't vote for our own idea, of course. So it's five votes for the cave – and the cave it will be. I'm glad – it's a great place really!'

'Is it? Let's go and see it straight away!' said Jack. 'It's not very far.'

'All right, come on then,' said Peter. 'We'll have a quick look, and then plan what to bring to it tomorrow. We'll settle into it at once.'

This was exciting. They all got up and went out into the bright sunshine. It was almost half-past six, and as warm as could be.

'This way,' said Peter, and led the way down his garden and through a gate into a field. His father owned the farmland at the back of the house, and it stretched away over the hills, the fields green with growing corn and root-crops.

Peter took them down a grassy path, past a pond with ducks on it, and then turned to the right towards the old quarry. Sand had been dug from it years ago, and it had then been abandoned. They all filed into the quarry and looked round.

Scamper ran in front. 'He'll show you,' said Peter. 'Just as he showed me and Janet this morning!' Scamper ran up to what looked like a rabbit path, over a little sandy hill, then down into a hollow behind. The others followed. Scamper stood waiting for them, his tail waving to and fro.

He ran through a gap in some thick bushes and disappeared. The others went through the gap too and looked for Scamper. He had gone!

'He's gone into the cave,' said Peter, grinning. 'You can see the entrance just there. It's all hung over with some plant that has sent long, trailing stems down, and has almost hidden the entrance to the cave. Come on – it's really quite exciting!'

[4]

In the cave

The Secret Seven crowded together to see the cave. There was no proper path to it, and they had to squeeze through close-growing bushes of bright yellow broom to get to it. The bushes grew almost up to the cave entrance.

'No wonder Janet and I never spotted this cave before,' said Peter. 'We've been in this old sand quarry heaps of times, but never found the cave. It was only because old Scamper disappeared and we went to look for him that we found it. We were standing here, calling him, when he suddenly appeared under the trailing leaves that hide the cave! Didn't you, Scamper?'

'Woof!' said Scamper, and ran into the

cave and back, as if to say, 'Do come on, it's a fine place!'

The trailing stems that hung down over the entrance certainly hid it very well. Peter pulled the greenery aside. 'It's like a curtain,' he said. 'Look – now you can see into the cave properly.'

Everyone bent their heads and looked in. It certainly was a fine cave!

'Nice and big, and with a lovely sandy floor!' said Jack. 'I don't see why you said it's not comfortable, Peter. Sand is lovely to sit on.'

'Oh well, I had to say *something* against it, as it was Janet's suggestion and mine,' said Peter.

By now they were all in the cave. Pam flung herself down on the sand. It was very soft indeed.

'Lovely!' she said. 'I'd like to sleep here in this sand. I could burrow my body down into it and make a lovely bed. It's a *wonderful* meeting-place, I think.'

'Nobody would EVER find it!' said George, looking round. 'It's a bit dark, that's the only thing. It's that green curtain over the entrance that makes it so dark.'

Janet obligingly held the curtain back, and the sun streamed into the cave.

'Fine!' said Colin. 'We can have the curtain back when we're just playing about, and draw it when we're having a secret meeting. Couldn't be better. A cave with a ready-made curtain!'

'And look, the cave has a rock roof, all uneven, high here and low there,' said Barbara. 'And there are rocky shelves round the walls; we can use those to put our things on. We'll bring all kinds of things here! I expect we'll have to use this cave all the Easter hols, so we'll make it a kind of home as well as a meeting-place, shall we?'

Everyone thought this was a very good idea. 'We'll bring the shed cushions here,' said Janet. 'And a box for a table.'

'And keep food here, and lemonade or orangeade,' said Jack. 'Won't it be fun?'

'Yes, and you'll have to be careful not to let Susie follow you here,' said Peter warningly. 'She'd just love to come here and mess things about, bring her silly, giggling friends with her too, I expect, and have a picnic or something in the middle of the cave.'

'I'll be very careful,' promised Jack. 'Well, I must say this is a brilliant place for the Secret Seven. Not too far away, perfectly secret, quite lonely, and our very own. Can any of us come here when we like, Peter? When there's not a meeting or anything planned? I'd love to come and read here by myself.'

'Yes. I don't see why this shouldn't be a kind of headquarters as well as a meeting-place,' said Peter. 'Anyone can come whenever they like, but please leave it tidy, and don't go and eat all the food we leave here!'

'Of course not,' said everyone at once.

'If we come alone and want something to eat we'll bring it ourselves,' said Colin, and everyone agreed.

'Now, let's see. We'll come tomorrow at half-past ten,' began Peter, but Jack interrupted before he could say any more.

'Oh, earlier than that, Peter! It's going to be fun; I'd like to come earlier. Can't we make it half-past nine?'

'No, because Janet and I have jobs to do for our father and mother,' said Peter. 'We'll say ten, if you like. We can get our jobs done by then, I expect.'

'I've got jobs to do as well,' said Pam. 'I always help Mother with the housework in the hols. So does Barbara.'

'Well, say ten,' repeated Peter. 'And bring what you can to make the cave comfortable and homely. Bring books if you like – the cave's quite dry – and games.'

Everyone was sorry to leave the exciting

cave. It really was a nice one, spacious, though the roof was not very high, and it was only in places that the Seven could stand upright – clean, with its floor of soft sand – and reaching back into a very nice, mysterious darkness, quite out of reach of the sunshine.

Peter held back the curtain of greenery till everyone had gone out. Then he let it drop into place and arranged it so that hardly a bit of the entrance showed. Nobody at all would ever guess there was a big cave behind it, going right into the hill beyond!

Scamper came out last of all, his tail wagging madly. He liked the cave. It was exciting. There was no smell of rabbits in it, which was disappointing, but it was good fun to pretend there was, and to scrabble hard at the sand with his front paws, and send it showering into the air!

The Seven all walked back to the gate at the bottom of Peter's garden, and then up the garden to the front gate. They said goodbye, and went off to their different homes, thinking exciting thoughts.

Susie met Jack as he came in, and looked at his sandy shoes.

'Where have you been?' she demanded. 'I've been looking for you everywhere. Where did you get that sand on your shoes?'

'Ask no questions, and I'll tell you no lies,' said Jack, pushing by her.

'You've been with the Secret Seven, I know you have,' said Susie, and she laughed. 'What's the password? Is it still Sugarmouse? Ha, ha – I tricked you nicely over that, didn't I?'

[5]

Settling in

Next day Peter and Janet felt very excited. They went down the garden to collect the old cushions they had in the shed. The gardener had put them into another shed, together with the boxes, sacks, and other things.

He was very busy repairing the old shed. The two children peeped inside. It would certainly be nice and clean when it was all finished.

'I'd rather have the cave for the holidays though,' said Peter, and Janet nodded.

They were very laden indeed as they made their way down to the quarry. Scamper carried a bone in his mouth. He knew quite well they were going to the cave, and he wanted to take something too!

Peter and Janet were there before the others. They drew aside the curtain of greenery and went in. The curtain fell behind them.

'Don't draw it back yet, till the others come,' said Peter. 'They'll have to give the password outside the curtain before we pull it back. Otherwise we'd never know who was coming in! But the password will tell us it's the Secret Seven.'

Janet set down the cushions. Peter put down the box he had brought. It was heavy, because he had filled it with all kinds of things. He began to unpack.

'Hand me the things,' said Janet. 'I'll arrange them nicely on these rocky shelves. There's no hole we can use for a cupboard, but that won't matter. Gosh, isn't this going to be fun?'

Peter looked at his watch. 'It's almost ten,' he said. 'You go on arranging things, and I'll wait just at the entrance, behind the curtain, and ask for the passwords. The sand outside is so soft that we shan't hear anyone coming. I must watch for them.'

Almost immediately there came a soft shuffle outside. 'Password,' said Peter, in a low voice.

'Easter-egg!' said Colin's voice. Peter pulled aside the curtain of greenery, and Colin came staggering in, carrying a big cardboard box. He collapsed on the soft, sandy floor.

'Gosh! I never knew books were so heavy! I've brought my whole set of "Famous Five" books to put on the shelves for anyone to borrow, and they've nearly dragged my arms out!'

'Oh, fine, there's one I want to read again,' said Peter, pleased. 'Find a nice even shelf of rock somewhere along the wall there, Colin, and put the books up neatly.'

A small cough came from outside the cave. Someone was waiting to be allowed in. 'Password!' said Peter, at once.

'Easter-egg!' said two voices together, and Peter lifted the green curtain. In came Pam and Barbara carrying parcels.

'Janet will see to those,' said Peter, taking up his post by the curtain again. Soon he heard the soft sound of feet coming quietly over the sand outside, and heard, too, the noise of people squeezing through the thick bushes of yellow broom.

'Password!' he said, and two voices answered together. 'Easter-egg!'

'Not so loud, idiots!' said Peter, and pulled aside the green curtain, grinning widely at Jack and George. He peered cautiously behind them.

'It's all right. I slipped off while Susie was at the bottom of our garden,' said Jack, staggering in. 'I've brought two bottles of juice and two bottles of water. Mother said I could, as her share towards the Secret Seven goings-on!'

'Goodo!' said Peter, pleased. He drew

back the curtain and tied it with a bit of string, so that the sunshine flooded into the cave. He looked all round outside to make sure that no one was about.

'I think we're absolutely safe and secret here,' he said. 'This quarry has been deserted for years, and I don't expect that anyone remembers there was ever a cave here.'

'Scamper would bark if anyone wandered near,' said Janet. 'Then we could quickly pull the curtain over the entrance and lie as quiet as anything!'

'Yes. Scamper would certainly warn us,' said Peter. 'Now, how are you all getting on?'

The cave was beginning to look quite cosy and furnished. The box-table was in the middle. Cushions were here and there on the sandy floor, ready for anyone to sit on. Arranged on the uneven ledges of the rocky wall were Colin's books and some of Jack's. Plastic cups had been neatly put in a row by

Janet, and on a wider ledge she had put Jack's bottles.

A tin stood in one corner. It had in it some of the food that the Seven had brought, and on another ledge stood a tin of boiled sweets, a packet of oatmeal biscuits, and two bars of chocolate brought by Pam. A small jar of potted crab paste stood next to a jar of home-made strawberry jam.

'It all looks very good,' said Peter approvingly. 'Very good indeed.'

'Yes. We've found places for everything,' said Janet, pleased. 'That corner over there belongs to Scamper, by the way, that's where he's buried the big bone he brought with him. Please don't disturb it, anyone. You can stop sitting on it, Scamper. I've told everyone it's your own special corner.'

Scamper still sat there, however. To him a bone was a very precious possession indeed, and he had to make *quite* sure that everyone understood it was *his* bone.

'I'm hungry after all this,' announced Jack. 'I vote we choose something to eat. We've got very well-filled cupboards!'

'I'll have a ginger bun,' said Colin. 'My mother made them yesterday. They're lovely. Let's begin with those.'

So there they sat, all the Secret Seven, happily munching ginger buns. The sun streamed in at the cave entrance, for the green curtain was still pulled back. What a lovely meeting-place – the best they had ever had!

Jack is very puzzled

The cave was a great success. On rainy days it was a wonderful place to lie in and read, or play games. Each of the Seven burrowed into the sand and made his or her own bed or hole. Each had a cushion for their head. The shelves were always kept stacked with papers and magazines, and with food and drink.

'We couldn't have found a better place,' said Colin. 'Jack, does Susie ever bother about where you disappear to for hours on end?'

'Goodness, yes,' said Jack. 'She keeps on and on about it. She knows our old shed is no longer a meeting-place, because she went to have a look at it. I have to be awfully careful not to let her follow me when I come here.

Yesterday I turned round and there she was, keeping to the bushes beside the road, hoping I wouldn't see her.'

'What did you do?' asked Pam.

'I turned a corner and went off to the sweet shop instead of coming here,' said Jack. 'I do hope she won't find our cave.'

'Let's go into the quarry and play hide-and-seek,' said Janet, getting up. 'The sun's out again, and I'm longing to stretch my legs.'

So off they all went. Jack was chosen to shut his eyes and count a hundred before he began looking. The cave was to be Home.

Jack stood by a tree at the other side of the quarry, counting nice and slowly. When he had counted a hundred, he looked round. Could he see anyone behind a bush, or lying in the lush grass nearby?

No – not one of the others was to be seen. He moved cautiously round his tree, keeping his eyes open for a sudden movement somewhere.

He glanced towards the cave, which he could just see between a gap in the broom bushes that hid it so well. Then he stared. Someone was slipping into the cave! Who was it? He just couldn't see.

That's not fair, thought Jack. They haven't given me a chance to find them. Well, I'll soon find out which of the Seven it is, and tell them what I think of them!

He saw a patch of blue nearby and recognised Pam's dress behind a bush. He rushed at her, but she escaped and ran squealing to the cave.

Then he found Barbara, Janet, and Scamper together, crouching behind a great hummock of sand. He ran to catch them and fell headlong over a tuft of grass. They rushed away, the girls squealing and Scamper barking.

He nearly caught Colin behind a tree, but Colin was too quick for him. Let's see – that only leaves one more, said Jack to himself.

The first one I saw going into the cave –
then the three girls – then Colin – myself –
and so there's just one more. It's Peter or
George.

He hunted here and there, and then suddenly fell over two giggling boys. It was Peter
and George, half-buried in the soft sand.
Jack grabbed at Peter and caught him, but
George escaped to the cave.

'I'm caught all right!' said Peter, grinning.
'I'll be "He" next. Let's call out to everyone
in the cave.'

'Wait a minute,' said Jack, looking
puzzled. 'There's something I don't understand. Let's go up to the cave.'

Peter went with him to the cave, where the
other five were waiting.

'What don't you understand?' asked Peter.

'Well, listen – first I saw someone slipping
into the cave immediately after I'd finished
counting,' said Jack, 'which wasn't really
fair. Then I found Pam, then Janet and

Barbara, then Colin, then you and George, Peter.'

'Well – what's puzzling you?' asked Peter.

'Just this – that makes *eight* of us, not counting Scamper,' said Jack. 'And what I want to know is, who was the eighth?'

They all counted. Yes, Jack was right. That made eight, not seven. Everyone said at once that they hadn't slipped into the cave before Jack discovered them.

'Well, who was that first person then, if it wasn't any of us?' said Jack, really puzzled. 'I tell you I saw somebody go into the cave before I discovered *any* of you. Who was it?'

Everyone began to look round uneasily. Peter pulled the green curtain back as far as he could, and the sunshine filled the cave, except for the dark places at the back.

'There's nobody here,' said Pam. 'Oh, Jack, do you suppose it could have been Susie?'

'I don't know. I only just saw *somebody*,

but I haven't any idea who it was,' said Jack. 'And look here, surely that somebody must still be in here! I found Pam almost immediately, and she rushed off to the cave. You didn't see anyone here, did you, Pam?'

'Of course not,' said Pam. 'If I'd seen Susie I would have been furious with her!'

Peter took down a torch from the shelf of rock nearby and switched it on. He flashed it towards the dark corners at the end of the cave. 'Come forth!' he said, in a hollow voice. 'Come forth, O wicked intruder!'

But nobody came. The far corners of the cave, now lit brilliantly by the torch, were quite empty.

'It's odd,' said Jack, frowning. 'Very odd. Give me the torch, Peter. I'll go and see if there's any corner or hole at the end of the cave that we haven't noticed.'

'Well, there isn't,' said Peter, giving him the torch. 'Janet and I had a good look when we first found the cave!'

All the same, Jack went to the far end and had a very good look round, flashing the torch everywhere. There seemed to be nowhere that anyone could hide.

He came back, still looking puzzled. 'Cheer up,' said Peter. 'You must have imagined someone, Jack. Anyway, *would* anyone come to that cave while we were all of us here, in plain view?'

'But that's just what we were not,' said Jack. 'We were playing hide-and-seek, and there wasn't a sound, and all of us, except me, were well hidden. Anybody coming here just then would not have heard or seen anything of us. They would have thought the place deserted.'

'Yes. I see what you mean,' said Peter. 'All the same, there's nobody here. So cheer up, Jack, and let's go on with the game. My turn to find you all. Go and hide!'

[7]

A real mystery

Nobody said any more about Jack's idea that someone had slipped into the cave. Jack began to think he really must have imagined it. Perhaps it was a shadow from a cloud or something? They all played the game of hide-and-seek again and again, and nobody saw mysterious people slipping into the cave any more!

'It's time to tidy up and go home,' said Peter, at last. 'What a mess we seem to make when we've been in the cave for even a short time!'

The girls shook up the cushions, and the boys gathered up the rubbish and put it into a bag to take home. Then Janet put the rest of the food back on the shelves, and tidied up Colin's set of 'Five' books.

'There!' she said. 'Everything tidy! If our mothers came and looked in they would be most astonished.'

They all laughed. They went out of the cave, and Peter pulled the green curtain carefully across. Then off they went home.

'Same time tomorrow!' called Peter, when they all said goodbye to him and Janet and Scamper at his front gate.

'No! You've forgotten – we're all going to bike over to Penton and see the circus come through,' said Colin. 'We're meeting at eleven at my house.'

'Oh, yes, how could I forget?' said Peter. 'We'll go to the cave after dinner tomorrow afternoon.'

Next day they had a good morning, watching the long circus procession passing through the little town of Penton. Then they biked back for their dinners, and, at various times, set off to the cave.

Pam and Barbara arrived first, Pam was

very pleased because her granny had given
her a tin of peppermints for the Secret Seven
to enjoy.

'I'll put them beside the other tins,' she
said. 'Hallo – look, Barbara, there's a tin on
the floor of the cave. Who do you suppose
knocked that down? We're the first here
today!'

'Perhaps it overbalanced,' said Barbara.

'And gosh, look – we left a whole bar of
chocolate, a very big one, just *here*,' said
Pam. 'I put it there myself. That's gone!'

'It's probably somewhere else,' said Barbara. Then she herself noticed something.
'Gosh, look – three of our cushions are
missing! Has somebody been here?'

'It's Susie,' said Pam frowning. 'That's
who it is. She didn't come with us to Penton
today, so she must have come here instead!
She has followed Jack sometime or other,
and found out our meeting-place. Bother
Susie!'

'Here are the others,' said Barbara. 'Let's tell them.'

They heard the password being murmured outside the cave. 'Easter-egg' – then the curtain was pushed aside and in came Colin and George.

'Susie's been here!' said Pam angrily. 'Look, there are cushions missing, and our big bar of chocolate is gone, and a tin was on the ground.'

'And look, those currant buns we were saving for today are nearly all gone!' said Barbara, opening a tin. 'Would you believe it!'

Soon Peter, Janet, and Jack arrived and were also told the news. 'But it needn't have been Susie,' said Peter, trying to be fair, though he felt perfectly certain it was. 'It could quite well have been a tramp.'

'He'd have taken lots more things,' said Pam. 'And what would he want with *cush-ions*! We might meet him down a lane carrying them, and we'd know he was the thief at once. No tramp would be as silly as that.'

'That's true,' said Peter. 'Well, Jack, you'll have to find out if it's Susie.'

'All right,' said Jack, looking troubled. 'I'll go now. But somehow I don't think it *is* Susie, you know. I can't help remembering that person, whoever it was, that I saw slipping into the cave yesterday.'

Jack went off to find Susie. The others each took a peppermint from the tin that Pam offered them, and settled down to read. Colin finished his book and went to get another. He gave an exclamation.

'One of my "Famous Five" books has gone! Has anyone borrowed it? It's *Five Go Down to the Sea.*'

Nobody had. 'I know it's not Jack,' said Colin. 'He's just finished reading it. Well, if that's Susie again I'll have something to say to her!'

Jack came back in about an hour. 'Easter-egg' he said, outside the cave, and Peter called him in.

'Well,' he said, throwing himself down on the sandy floor. 'I've had an awful time. Susie says she's never been *near* our new meeting-place, she says she doesn't even know where it is! She flew into such a temper when I accused her of coming and taking things, that Mother heard her, and came to see what was the matter.'

'Oh, bother!' said Peter. 'You might have kept your mother out of this. What happened next?'

'Mother made me tell where our meeting-place is,' said poor Jack, looking really miserable. 'I couldn't help it, Peter, really I couldn't. She *made* me.'

There was silence. Everyone knew that it was wrong, and also quite impossible, to refuse to tell mothers anything they wanted to know. But to give away their wonderful new meeting-place! How truly shocking.

'Was Susie there when you told?' asked Peter.

'Yes,' said Jack. 'She was, and she said she was jolly well coming to find the cave and make a real mess of it! I don't think she did come here this morning. She was with Jeff all the time in the garden. Mother said so.'

'Well then, who did?' said Peter, puzzled. 'It's a strange thief who comes and takes three *cushions*!'

There was a silence. Pam glanced round the cave fearfully. Who was it who came here? Jack had seen someone yesterday, and now the someone had come again today. WHO was it?

'Now that Susie knows about our cave, I think that someone must be here on guard whenever we're not here,' said Peter. 'I mean – we can't let Susie come and mess everything up. I can quite see that if it wasn't her who came and took the things this morning, she must be really furious with us for thinking it was.'

'I wouldn't be surprised if she brought Jeff with her and turned the whole place upside down now,' said Jack gloomily. 'You don't know Susie like I do.'

'Well, let's make things jolly unpleasant for them if they do come,' said George. 'Let's balance a jug of water on that ledge over the green curtain. As soon as the curtain is moved, the jug will overbalance and pour water all over them.'

Pam giggled. 'Yes. Let's do that!'

'And let's do what my cousin once did to someone he didn't like,' said Colin. 'He got a reel of cotton and wound it all over and across the entrance to our summer-house – and he dipped it in honey first! Then when this awful boy walked into the summer-house, he walked right through the sticky threads and thought that an enormous spider's web had caught him!'

'How horrible!' said Pam, shuddering. 'To have sticky thread all over you like that!'

'Susie would hate it,' said Barbara. 'She loathes getting caught in spider thread. But who's got cotton or honey? Nobody here!'

'I can run indoors and get a reel of silk from my work-box,' said Janet, 'and there's some honey in a jar in our kitchen, I know. But aren't we being rather horrid to Susie?'

'No, Susie will only get caught in our tricks if she finds the cave and comes to turn it upside down,' said Pam. 'It will be her own fault if she gets caught. Nobody else's.'

'It's no good being soft-hearted with Susie,' said Jack gloomily. 'Actually, sometimes I think she's cleverer than any of us!'

Janet ran off to get the honey and the reel of silk. Barbara complained because her cushion was gone and she now had nothing to rest her head on.

'I suppose whoever took our cushions did it for some kind of silly joke,' she said. 'And probably threw them into the bushes some-where.'

'I'll go and look,' said Colin, and got up. But the cushions were nowhere to be seen, and he soon came back. Janet came with him, having got the reel and the honey.

'We'll get the tricks ready when we go home to tea,' said Peter. 'I'll slip up after tea to make sure that no one's been into the cave, and I'll come last thing at night too.'

Just before they left they arranged the booby-traps. Janet ran the grey silk thread through the sticky honey, and the boys wound it back and forth across the entrance to the cave, twisting it round the plants that lined the edges of the cave entrance from top to bottom.

'There!' said Peter, at last. 'No one can get in without getting covered with thin, sticky threads! And what a shock they'll get too, when they draw back the curtain and get swamped with water from that jug! I've balanced it very carefully, so that at the slightest pulling back of the green curtain the water will pour out!'

Everyone giggled and wished they could be there to see the booby-traps catch any intruder. 'I hope Jeff comes with Susie, I can't bear him,' said Jack. 'And shan't I laugh if Susie comes back sticky and wet! Come on, let's go.'

After tea Peter went up to the cave to examine the booby-traps. They were still there! The jug of water, half-hidden by leaves, was still in place, and he could see the grey, sticky threads gleaming behind the green curtain.

'Susie and Jeff haven't been yet,' he told Janet, when he got back. 'I'll slip up again just before it gets dark and have another look.'

So up he went once more to the cave, but again the booby-traps were still there, untouched. Susie won't come now, he thought. I'll be up here before nine o'clock tomorrow morning and watch out for her in case she comes then.

[8]

Scamper is a help

Jack came to see Peter just before nine the next day. 'I came to tell you that Susie's not been near the cave,' he told Peter. 'I kept an eye on her all yesterday evening and this morning. She's gone off to her music lesson now, so we're safe till twelve o'clock anyhow.'

'Right,' said Peter. 'Well, help me with the few jobs I have to do, and then we'll go up with Janet and Scamper. We'll try to get there just before the others come.'

So at five to ten, Peter, Janet, Scamper, and Jack made their way to the quarry and then up to the cave.

They looked up to where the jug was so carefully balanced on a ledge, and grinned.

'I'll get it,' said Jack, and climbed up to remove it.

'We'll have to break these threads ourselves,' said Janet. 'What a waste of booby-traps, wasn't it? Ooh, be careful, you'll get honey all over you!'

They broke the threads as carefully as possible, so as not to get themselves sticky, and went into the cave. And then they stood there in astonishment, gazing round as if they could not believe their eyes!

The tins were all opened – and emptied! Some were flung on the floor. Two more of the cushions had gone. A bottle of orangeade had disappeared, and so had a bottle of water. The tin of peppermints had completely vanished, and also some more books. A torch that Colin had left on a shelf had gone too.

'But – but – how could anyone get *in*?' stammered Peter, utterly astonished. 'Our booby-traps were still there – those threads were quite unbroken. NOBODY could have come in, and yet look at this. I don't like it. There's something very strange going on in this cave – and I just don't – like – it!'

The three children felt scared. It was quite clear that *no one* had gone into the cave, because the sticky silk threads would certainly have been broken. But how could their belongings have been taken, and their tins emptied, if no one had been in the cave?

'You know,' said Jack, looking all round him fearfully, 'you know, Peter, I was quite certain I saw somebody slipping into the cave that time we played hide-and-seek. You kept saying I must have imagined it, but I didn't.'

'Well, certainly *somebody's* about, somebody who likes eating and drinking,' said Peter. 'And if he didn't get into our cave from the *outside*, he must know a way in from the *inside*!'

'But that's silly too,' said Janet. 'We know

there's no way into the cave from the inside.
We've had a jolly good look.'

'Scamper seems very interested in the cave
this morning,' said Jack. 'Look at him sniffing and nosing round.'

Scamper certainly was interested. He ran
here and there excitedly, giving little barks
and whimpers, as if to say, 'I could tell you
such a lot if only I could speak!'

He ran over to the place where he had
buried his bone, dug it up, and carefully took
it to another corner and buried it there. Peter
laughed.

'He's afraid our visitor might find his bone
– see how deep he's burying it this time! Hey,
Scamper, you're sending sand all over us!'

Janet looked round at the untidy cave
with its empty tins and scattered books.
Tears came into her eyes. 'I made it all so
nice,' she said. 'And we had such a lot of
good food here. WHO is this horrible visitor
who comes when we're not here and steals

like this? Where does he come from? How does he get here if he doesn't come in at the entrance?'

'Let's look all round the cave again, very, very carefully to see if there's another entrance somewhere,' said Jack. 'There might be a small hole that someone could wriggle through, covered with sand.'

They looked thoroughly, Scamper sniffing too. But no, no matter how Scamper sniffed all round and about, or how the children dug here and there to find a hole under the rocky walls, nothing was found that would help to solve the mystery.

'And a very strange mystery it is too,' said Peter. 'I said I didn't like it, and I don't. I vote we clear up this cave and find another meeting-place. It's going to be no fun if we keep having our things stolen and messed about by some unknown visitor.'

'Yes. *I* don't feel as if I want to be here any more either,' said Janet. 'It's a shame. It's such a good place. Well, the others will be along soon, so let's just clear up a bit, and we'll tell them when they come.'

It wasn't long before the others came, all four of them, chattering and laughing as they walked through the old quarry.

As soon as they arrived at the cave, Peter told them what had happened. They stared at his grave face and listened in astonishment to what he told them.

'It's very odd,' said George. 'I don't understand it. Taking food – and cushions – and books! It sounds like someone hiding somewhere and needing food, and something soft to lie on.'

'If one or two of us hid here in the cave tonight, we might see whoever it is that comes,' said Colin.

There was a silence. Nobody liked the idea at all. This mysterious visitor didn't sound a very nice person to lie in wait for.

'Well,' said Peter at last, 'I'm no coward,

but considering that there really isn't any place in this cave that we could hide in without being seen almost at once, I don't see much point in your suggestion, Colin. I mean the intruder, whoever he is, would probably see *us* before we spotted him. Anyway, I don't like the sound of him.'

'Nor do I,' said Jack. 'I vote we clear out of here and have another meeting-place. What's the sense of bringing stuff here and having it taken as soon as our back's turned?'

They began to clear up the cave. It was really very sad. Scamper watched them in surprise. Why were they looking so miserable? Why were they packing up everything? Well, he'd certainly better get his bone then! He couldn't leave that behind if everyone was leaving the cave!

He ran over to the corner where he had buried it. His sharp nose sniffed something else not far off on a low ledge of rock. Did it belong to the children? It didn't really smell like any of them. Scamper could always tell what shoe or glove belonged to any of the Seven just by sniffing it!

Scamper sniffed at this thing on the ledge, and then picked it up in his mouth. Perhaps it did belong to one of the children after all. He ran with it to Peter and dropped it at his feet with a little bark.

'Hello, Scamper, what is it?' said Peter. He bent down and picked up a small, dirty notebook with a frayed elastic band round it. 'Anyone own this?' he asked, holding it up.

Nobody did. Jack came up, excited.

'Peter! It might have been dropped by our strange visitor! Look inside!'

Peter slipped off the elastic band and opened the little notebook. His eyes suddenly shone. 'Yes!' he said, in a low voice. 'It *does* belong to our visitor – and here's his name – look. Wow, this *is* a find! He dropped it when he came raiding our cave last night!'

They all crowded round him in excitement. Peter's finger pointed to a name scribbled at the front of the notebook.

'Albert Tanner,' he said. 'He must be our mysterious visitor. Albert Tanner! Who can he be? Well, we'll find out *somehow*!'

An exciting plan

'Let's clear out of here quickly,' said Colin, in a low voice, looking nervously all round the cave. 'If Albert Tanner, whoever he is, is anywhere near, as he does seem to be, we don't want him to know we've found his notebook. We're all ready to go. Let's scoot off quickly, and examine the notebook in secret.'

'Good idea,' said Peter. 'Ready everyone? Come on then! Scamper, to heel!'

They left the cave and went out into the bright sunshine, each carrying a load. The tins, alas, were now empty, and very light to carry. Half Colin's *Famous Five* books were gone, so he hadn't a great load, either. Most of the magazines had disappeared too. Evidently their mysterious visitor was quite a reader!

They went through the quarry and into Peter's garden. 'We'll go to the summer-house, I think,' said Peter. 'It's not very comfortable, but at least we can talk in secret there.'

Soon they were all sitting on the little bench that ran round the old summer-house, with Scamper panting on the floor in a patch of warm sunshine.

Peter took the worn notebook out of his pocket and opened it. The others crowded as near as possible to see what was in it. Peter turned over the pages.

'Albert Tanner has written his name in the front as you know,' he said. 'Which was kind of him, I must say – we at least know the *name* of our visitor now! There doesn't seem much else in the book, actually. Just a few notes of money and various dates, and a few words scribbled here and there. Let's see – yes – "potatoes, turnips, tomatoes, flour", just a shopping list, I suppose.'

He turned over a page or two. 'Another shopping list, and some figures jotted down. It doesn't seem as if this notebook is going to be of any use at all!'

Jack took it from him and looked through it too. At the back was a folded-in piece of leather to hold paper money. Peter hadn't noticed it. Jack slipped his fingers in to see if anything could be there.

Yes, a slip of paper, small and torn, with something scribbled on it in a different handwriting from Albert Tanner's.

'Look here!' said Jack. 'This was in the back of the notebook. See what it says? It's a note to Albert Tanner.'

'What does it say?' asked Janet, excited. 'Anything of use to us?'

'It's just scribble,' said Jack, screwing up his eyes. 'It says, "Daren't write it. Jim knows the place. He'll tell you. Meet him on post office seat 8.30 p.m., 15th. Ted."'

'The 15th! That's today,' said Peter. 'Read

it again, it's evidently an important message, but how mysterious! What's this "place" Jim is going to tell Albert? My word, if only we could know it! We could go to the "place" Jim says and have a good snoop round.'

A little feeling of excitement began to stir in everyone. Colin caught hold of Peter's sleeve.

'I'll go to the post office seat tonight and sit there. Perhaps I shall see this "Jim" and hear what he says to Albert. I shall *see* Albert too!'

There was a silence, and the excitement suddenly grew stronger. 'A few of us should go,' said Peter. 'Not just you.'

'You can't,' said Janet. 'You're going to see "*Westward Ho!*" at the cinema. Mother's taking us both. And George is coming too, don't you remember?'

'Bother!' said Peter. 'Well, we can't get out of that without giving the whole thing away. Colin, you and Jack must go. And for goodness' sake listen hard and hear what's being said!'

'Right,' said Colin, thrilled. 'Can you come, Jack?'

'Oh yes!' said Jack. 'And what about us shadowing Albert and Jim, Peter? One of us could follow Albert, and the other one could follow Jim. It might be useful to know where Jim lives, and I must say I'd like to follow Albert if he goes back to the cave!'

'A jolly good idea,' said Peter. 'I only wish I could come too. But it's no good. I begged and begged to go to "*Westward Ho!*" and I can't get out of it now.'

They pored over the little note again, written in a bad handwriting, hurried and careless. Peter read it out aloud once more.

'Daren't write it. Jim knows the place. He'll tell you. Meet him on post office seat 8.30 p.m., 15th. Ted.'

'Would there be something hidden in this "place" that is in the note, do you think?' said Janet.

'Yes. Probably,' said Peter, thinking hard.

'And if it's hidden, it's valuable. And if it's valuable it may be stolen goods.'

'Yes. Goods stolen by Ted, whoever he is, and hidden away!' said Colin. 'Or stolen by Ted *and* Albert – and Ted hid them – then got caught, perhaps, and went to prison. And now he wants Albert to find them.'

Everyone laughed. 'You've made quite a story of it!' said Jack. 'I don't expect it's anything like that really. All the same, as soon as we know the place we'll certainly go there – if only we can get there before Albert does!'

'Yes, that's not going to be so easy!' said Peter. 'Maybe Albert will go there at once.'

'I hope he does!' said Colin. 'We'll be shadowing him, and he'll lead us right to this mysterious "place", wherever it is!'

'I wish I was going to be with you tonight,' said Peter longingly. 'It's an adventure, you know, and they don't come very often. I WISH I was going to share it!'

[10]

What happened at half-past eight

Colin met Jack that evening at eight o'clock outside the post office. It was dark, and there was no moon. They spoke together in low voices as they went over to the wooden seat nearby.

'What shall our plans be?' said Colin. 'The seat is just by that big chestnut tree. Shall we hide behind the tree, or get under the seat, or what?'

'We mustn't both of us be in the same place,' said Jack. 'Otherwise if the men see us and send us off, we'll neither of us hear a word. I vote one of us gets *behind* the tree, and the other *up* the tree!'

'That's a very good idea,' said Colin. 'You'd

better climb up the tree. I've got a stiff knee, and it's bandaged. I fell down our cellar steps today, and Mother made a tremendous fuss, and I was afraid she'd make me rest in bed or something! I nearly had a fit, thinking I might not be able to come this evening!'

'All right. I'll climb the tree,' said Jack. 'But I'd better do it now, before anyone comes. There's nobody about at all. I'll stand on the back of the seat, and you can give me a leg-up to that big branch that overhangs the seat.'

It wasn't long before Jack was perched in the thick branches of the chestnut tree. Colin went behind the tree and leaned against the trunk, waiting. The church clock chimed a quarter past eight. Colin's heart began to beat faster – this *was* fun!

Ten minutes went by, and then someone came up. No, two people, arm-in-arm. Colin stiffened and held his breath. The two people passed talking together. Then someone else walked by smartly with a dog.

And then somebody came slouching along in rubber-soled shoes, a shadowy someone who kept out of the light of the street-lamps. He sat down on the seat, and Colin almost stopped breathing!

Jack peered down cautiously from the tree, but it was so dark that he could make out very little except that the man was wearing a cap.

Another shadowy figure appeared from across the road, walking silently. It joined the man on the seat. The two men sat a little apart, saying nothing, and the listening boys held their breath again.

After a few minutes of silence, the first man spoke. 'You're Albert. That's right, isn't it?'

But, before Albert could even nod his head, something happened that made the two men almost jump out of their skins.

Colin sneezed! He always had a very loud sneeze indeed, but this one was tremendous! He didn't even know it was coming, and it gave him almost as much of a shock as it gave the two men!

'A . . . WHOOOOOSH – OOO!'

In a trice Albert had whipped behind the tree and got hold of the startled Colin. He held him in a grip of iron. 'What are you doing here? Hiding behind this tree?'

He shook poor Colin until the boy felt as if his head would fly off. The other man came round the tree too.

'It's only a kid,' he said. 'Let him go. We don't want any noise here.'

Colin got a blow on the head and went staggering away, almost falling. Albert ran at him again, and the boy fled for his life, terrified. Jack, up in the tree, felt very scared too. Should he go to Colin's rescue? No, by the time he'd got down the tree it would be too late. Ah, Colin had run away, so he was all right. Jack clung to the branch, trembling a little.

The men stood under the tree together.

'Better clear off,' said the first man, in a low voice to Albert.

'You've got something to tell me,' said Albert.

'Yes. The scarecrow!' said his companion, lowering his voice. 'That's where it is. Look by the scarecrow.'

'Thanks,' said Albert, and slouched off silently, and was soon lost in the shadows. Jack wished Colin could have shadowed him. *He* certainly couldn't shadow Albert, because it would take him a minute or two to get cautiously down the tree. Perhaps he could follow the first man, though.

By the time Jack was safely down the tree both men had completely disappeared. Jack made off as quickly as he could, feeling decidedly scared. Was Colin all right? He'd better go to his house and see if he could find out, without letting anyone else know why he had come!

When he arrived at Colin's house he saw a

light in Colin's bedroom window. Good! He threw up a pebble and hit the window-pane first time. The window was opened cautiously, and Colin's head came out.

'Colin! It's me, Jack! Are you all right?' called Jack, in a low voice.

'Yes. Quite. That man gave me a jolly good box on the ear, but I got home all right, and no one saw me coming in. What about you? Did you hear anything?'

'Yes, but nothing *really* helpful,' said Jack. 'What a terrific sneeze that was of yours, Colin!'

'Yes, my goodness. I thought I—' began Colin, and then drew his head in quickly. Jack heard him speaking to someone in his bedroom, and ran out of the gate as quickly as he could.

The *scarecrow*! he thought. What does that mean? *I* don't know! Perhaps Peter will. Gosh, I can hardly wait until tomorrow morning to tell him!

[11]

Off they go again!

The meeting in the summer-house the next morning was quite exciting. Peter and Janet and Scamper waited impatiently for Jack and Colin to come. Pam and Barbara came together as usual, then came George, and last of all Colin and Jack.

'Sorry we're a bit late,' said Jack. 'I went to call for Colin. His leg's still stiff so he couldn't walk very fast, though you ran fast enough last night, didn't you, Colin?'

Colin grinned. He had a bruise on the left cheekbone near his ear, where he had been struck the night before. He felt rather proud of it.

'We've got some news,' said Jack, feeling extremely important as he looked round at the expectant faces of the others.

'Well, hurry up and tell us then,' said Peter impatiently. 'Did those two men meet? What did you hear?'

'Tell it all from the beginning,' begged Janet. 'I like to know every single thing so that I can see it in my mind's eye.'

'All right,' said Jack. 'Well, Colin and I met by the post office at eight o'clock, and the men came at half-past. Colin hid behind a tree, and I climbed up into it.'

'Well done,' said Peter approvingly.

'Just as the men were beginning to talk Colin did the most TERRIFIC sneeze you ever heard,' said Jack. 'Honestly, I nearly fell out of the tree!'

'Gosh!' said Janet. 'Whatever happened then?'

'The men ran round the tree and found poor old Colin, and that bruise on his cheek is where he got hit,' said Jack. Everyone gazed in awe at Colin's bruise, and he felt very proud indeed.

'He had to run for his life, and there was I, stuck up the tree,' went on Jack, enjoying himself immensely. 'I can tell you, it was quite an adventure! Well, then the men spoke in low voices again, but I managed to hear the important thing.'

'What was it?' demanded Peter. 'You're so long-winded. Get to the point.'

'The first man – he must have been the Jim mentioned in the letter – he said "*The scarecrow*!"' said Jack, lowering his voice just as the men had done. '"The scarecrow! That's where it is!" he said. "The scarecrow!" Then the two men went off, and I hadn't time to shadow them because I was up the tree.'

'You did very well,' said Peter. 'Extremely well! It was a pity about Colin's sneeze. Still, you heard the main thing, Jack – and that was the word "scarecrow".'

'What does it mean, though?' asked Jack. 'Do *you* know? Does it mean a *real* scarecrow?'

'No. There's a tiny inn called "The Scarecrow" up on the common,' said Peter. 'I've often passed it when I've been in the car with my father. We'll go up there and snoop round. I bet that's where something is hidden, loot from some robbery, probably.'

'Oh, yes, *I* remember seeing that inn too, and thinking what an odd name it had,' said Janet. 'Peter, let's go *now*! Before Albert gets away with anything!'

'Yes. We'd certainly better go now, this very minute!' said Peter. 'We may find Albert there, digging away in some corner of the garden. It would be very interesting to see what he digs up!'

Everyone felt the delicious surge of excitement that always came over them when adventure was in the air. 'Get your bikes,' ordered Peter. 'Colin, is your knee too stiff to bike, do you think?'

'I can pedal all right with one leg,' said Colin, who wasn't going to be left out of this morning's excitement for anything. 'Come on, let's get our bikes, those of you who didn't come on them.'

'Meet at the crossroads by the old barn,' said Peter. 'Wait for each other. Then we'll all set off together. We're really on to something now!'

George was the only one who had come on a bike. The others set off to get theirs. Peter and Janet fetched their two from the shed, and set off with George to the crossroads, Scamper running excitedly behind them. He knew when adventure was about, he always knew!

Soon everyone was at the crossroads, even Colin, who could only pedal with one leg. Jack came last, looking hot and cross.

'What's up?' asked Janet, seeing how upset he looked. 'Did you get into trouble at home about anything?'

'No. It's Susie,' said Jack, with a groan. 'She says that she and Jeff went up to our cave this morning, you know I had to tell Mother about it in front of Susie, and when she saw we'd gone, she and Jeff decided to have it for their meeting-place! Isn't that maddening?'

'Well, let them if they want to!' said Peter. 'Much good may it do them! Albert will probably visit them as he did us and take their things! Serve them right!'

'I wonder how Albert gets into the cave if he doesn't use our entrance!' said Janet. 'We know he used it once, because Jack saw him that time, when we were playing hide-and-seek. But he didn't use it when he robbed us of all those things. Those silk threads at the entrance weren't broken, you remember!'

'I imagine that our dear friend Albert may be somewhere at the inn called "*The Scarecrow*"!' said Peter. 'He probably won't be using the cave much more if he finds what he's looking for!'

'Look, there it is – "*The Scarecrow*"!' said Pam, riding ahead. 'What a funny old inn, hundreds of years old, I should think. Come on, everybody – isn't this EXCITING!'

[12]

The Scarecrow Inn

The Secret Seven came near to the old inn. It was certainly a strange place, almost tumble-down. Outside a sign swung in the wind, creaking dismally. On it was painted a scarecrow in a field, and printed on it in big letters was the name.

'The Scarecrow,' said Peter, leaping off his bicycle. 'Here we are. Look out for Albert, everyone!'

They leaned their bicycles against a hedge and walked over to the inn. No one was about. The whole place looked completely deserted.

'But there must be somebody about!' said Colin. 'Look, there are a few hens pecking around.'

They went right up to the old inn. 'It seems to be shut,' said Peter, puzzled. 'Yes, look, there are bars across the windows and across the front door too, wooden bars, nailed on.'

'It must be closed down,' said Jack. 'Let's go round to the back. We can ask for a drink of water, or how to get to Penton, or something like that.'

So they all went round to the back door of the inn. A woman was in a little yard there, hanging out some washing, an old, grey-haired woman with a very disagreeable face.

'Er, could we have a drink of water, please?' asked Peter, in his politest voice.

'There's the well. Help yourself,' said the woman.

'Thank you. Is the inn closed now?' asked Peter.

'Yes. Been closed for months,' said the old woman, pegging up a sheet. 'I just caretake, and it's a lonely job up here on the common. You're the first people I've spoken to for about six weeks, except for the milkman and the grocer's boy.'

'Oh, then you don't know anyone called Albert, I suppose?' asked Peter, as innocently as he could.

'Now, don't you be cheeky,' said the woman angrily. 'Who told you my old man was called Albert? You call him Mr Larkworthy, and mind your manners. See, there he is. I'll send him after you if you're cheeky!'

The Secret Seven saw an old bent man coming out of the inn with a stick in his hand, on which he leaned heavily. Goodness, they hadn't meant to be cheeky! How could they have guessed that the old woman's husband was called Albert?

'We didn't mean your husband,' said Peter hurriedly. 'We really didn't. We're just looking for someone called Albert that we thought we might see here this morning.'

'Well, I won't have any cheek from children,' said the old woman. 'You clear off, now, before I tell my husband to chase you.'

The Seven went away slowly, taking a good look at the little place as they went. They walked to their bicycles by the hedge.

'What do you think, Peter?' asked Jack. 'Do you suppose Albert came here at all?'

'No,' said Peter. 'We're on the wrong track. I think that cross old woman was speaking the truth. She probably hasn't seen anyone here for weeks! Gosh, I did feel awful when she said her husband's name was Albert! No wonder she thought we were cheeky!'

'I had a good look at that little garden,' said George. 'And it's quite plain that nobody has been digging in it to get anything buried there. Nothing but enormous weeds.'

'Yes. I had a look too,' said Peter. 'No, we're on the wrong track, as I said. The thing is, what do we do next? If only we knew where Albert was at this moment, it would be a great help!'

'It might not be,' said Jack, with a grin. 'He might be scaring Jeff and Susie in our cave!'

'I hope he is,' said Peter grimly. 'Just like those two to try to annoy us!'

'What are we going to do now?' asked Janet. 'Peter, do you suppose it's a *real* scarecrow we have to look for?'

Peter considered. 'Yes, it might be. I was so sure that the old inn was the place meant, that I didn't really think about proper scarecrows. But we can't go chasing over the countryside looking for all the scarecrows in the fields!'

'Yes, we can,' said Colin. 'Quite easily. All we've got to do is to separate, and bike all over the place, and whenever we see a scarecrow, get off and see if anyone has been disturbing the ground by it. I *bet* whatever is hidden is well dug-in beside a scarecrow.'

'Yes. It would be such a good place if the thief wanted to get the loot again,' said Peter. 'I mean, if stolen goods were hidden in a field in the ordinary way, they couldn't be marked in case anyone wondered what the mark was for. A stick or a post or something would call attention to the place and make the farmer examine it. But a scarecrow is a *natural* mark and anything hidden beneath it wouldn't be found until the field was reaped!'

'Yes. And the thief meant to get it before that, as we know!' said George. 'Well, shall we go scarecrow-hunting?'

'Yes,' said Peter, getting on his bicycle. 'But look out for farmers. They mightn't be too pleased to see us walking all over their fields to get to a scarecrow!'

They all rode off together, Peter calling out orders as they went.

'You take the west road, Colin and Jack. You the east, Pam and Barbara. You take the north, George, and Janet and I will turn at the crossroads and take the south. We shall cover most of the countryside then. Meet at half-past two this afternoon in the summer-house.'

Off they all went. 'Scarecrow-hunting!' said Jack to Colin. 'What a game! I do wonder how many scarecrows we shall find!'

The Seven had a strange time, hunting for scarecrows! Pam and Barbara found a most fearsome one in the middle of a field, his coat flapping like mad in the wind.

They went to examine him, but as the soil was quite hard all round him they knew that nothing had been hidden and dug up beside *him*! So off they went to find another.

Colin and Jack found two. One was in an allotment, and although they were sure that it couldn't be the one they were looking for, they went up to him all the same, and examined the ground nearby.

A man came into the allotment with a spade over his shoulder. When he saw the two boys there he shouted at them angrily:

'You clear off, you two! These allotments are private. Are you the kids who've been taking broccoli from here?'

'No!' shouted the two boys. 'We were just having a look at the old scarecrow.'

'I'll scarecrow you if you come here again!' yelled the man, and Colin and Jack fled for their bicycles. The next scarecrow they found was in a field of young wheat, and no sooner had they walked over the field to the scarecrow than a farmer appeared with a dog. The boys just had time to make sure that the earth round the scarecrow was undisturbed before the dog flew at them.

'Ha! He'll bite you next time!' called the farmer, as the boys leapt on their bicycles.

'I don't think I like this scarecrow-hunting much,' said Colin, whose stiff leg was hurting him. 'That's twice we've had to run, and I just can't bend my knee properly.'

George, cycling quickly up and down country roads, thought he spied a scarecrow at the end of a field. He jumped off his bicycle and squeezed through the hedge – only to face a surprised and angry farm-labourer, hoeing vigorously.

'Oh – sorry – I thought you were a scare-crow,' said George very foolishly, backing away through the hedge. The farm-labourer, angry at being called a scarecrow, flung a clod of earth at George. It shattered into bits all over him. George spat some out of his mouth.

'Phoo! That was a good shot on his part!' said George, riding away. 'I don't know that I like this scarecrow business much!'

Peter and Janet had examined four scare-crows, for their particular roads ran between big farms, and great fields lay on either side. One scarecrow had thrilled Janet because a thrush had built a nest in the dented crown of the old scarecrow's hat. Peter could hardly get her away from it!

The other three they had found were not interesting, and quite plainly no one had been into the field to disturb the earth near any of the scarecrows.

Peter felt disheartened as he rode home

beside Janet. 'All those scarecrows and not one of them any good to us,' he complained. 'I only hope the others have found the right one.'

They got home just in time for their dinner. Their mother looked in horror at their shoes, which were covered in mud from the soil in two very wet fields they had walked over.

'Where *have* you been?' she said. 'And what in the world were you doing to get your shoes so filthy? Take them off at once, and leave them outside.'

'We went to look at scarecrows,' said Janet, 'and we found one with a thrush's nest in his hat! That's how we got our shoes so dirty. But we'll clean them ourselves.'

'You should go and see the scarecrow old James has put up in the oat-field,' said her father, who was already at the table. 'He tells me it's got a robin's nest in each pocket!'

'But how did he know?' said Janet in astonishment. 'He's almost blind, poor old man – he can't even see the clouds now, to tell him the weather.'

'Well, he's not too blind to see that somebody had been walking over his precious oat-field,' said her father. 'He followed the footsteps, and they led him right to the scarecrow – and that's how he found the two robins' nests in the pockets!'

Peter pricked up his ears at once. 'Somebody walking over our oat-field to the scarecrow?' he said. 'Who, Dad – and why?'

'Goodness knows,' said his father. 'There are plenty of foolish townspeople who think they can walk all over growing fields! It was one of them, I expect.'

But Peter felt sure it was Albert! He looked at his mother. He really must go and see! 'Er – please could I just go quickly and look at those robins' nests?' he said desperately.

His mother looked at him in amazement. 'What – *now*? Just as dinner's ready? Don't be silly, dear. The nests won't fly away –

they'll be there after dinner!'

Peter looked at Janet, who had read his thoughts. 'WHY didn't we think of our own scarecrow!' she blurted out. 'We see it from our bedroom windows each day. We—'

Peter gave her a sharp kick under the table, and she stopped at once. Goodness, she had nearly given the game away!

'Why all this sudden interest in scarecrows?' inquired her mother. 'I hope it soon wears off. I can't allow you to get your shoes like that again.'

Peter and Janet longed for dinner to be over. As soon as they were allowed to go, they shot out into the garden, and slipped on their dirty shoes.

'It was *our* scarecrow we should have looked at!' said Peter. 'I could kick myself! Come on – let's go now and examine the soil round it. We'll take a fork, in case we may find something, though I'm afraid that Albert has got there first. Hurry up!'

[13]

Everything seems dull now

Peter and Janet ran down the garden and out of the gate at the bottom. Round the potato-field and over a stile they went, and there was the oat-field, its green rows as bright as emerald!

In the middle of it stood the scarecrow put up by old James. He was a fine one, and wore one of James's old hats, cocked over on one side. He wore a ragged red jersey and an old tweed coat with sagging pockets. A robin flew out of one of them as the children went near.

The scarecrow's ragged trousers flapped in the wind against his two wooden legs. His head was a turnip in which old James had scraped eyes and mouth. He seemed to be grinning at them as they came up, and the wind shook him and made him jig to and fro.

But Peter and Janet didn't look at the scarecrow, or even at the robins' nests in the sagging pockets. They looked at the ground around his wooden legs.

And Peter gave a deep groan that really might have come from the old scarecrow! 'We *are* too late, Janet. Look, someone's been here. There are footprints all around and about, not only old James's hobnailed ones, but somebody with rubber-soled shoes – Albert's!'

'Yes,' said Janet, her eyes on the ground. 'And the soil has been well dug up. Something was hidden here, beside the old scarecrow. Oh, Peter, WHY didn't we look here first?'

'It wouldn't have been any good,' said Peter gloomily. 'I expect Albert came last night. He wouldn't come digging here in the daytime. He knew which scarecrow was meant, of course. We didn't! And all the time it was our own scarecrow!'

'Just dig round a bit and see if there's anything left,' said Janet.

'There won't be,' said Peter dolefully. 'I expect whatever it was was in a bag, a strong bag too, to resist the damp.' He dug about with his fork, but brought up nothing except a surprised worm. '*Bother!*' he said. 'I was so excited about this scarecrow business. Now we're too late, Albert has got the stuff, whatever it was, and will be off and away.'

'Yes, I suppose he will,' said Janet dismally. 'I wouldn't be surprised if he knew that it was hidden in this district and that was why he came and hid in our cave, so as to be on the spot to speak to that other man, what was his name? Jim? And to get the stuff easily.'

'I think you're absolutely right, Janet,' said Peter. 'And if you are, the stolen stuff, or whatever it was, must have *come* from this district too. I wonder if there have been any robberies lately.'

They had a look at the two cosy robins' nests, both of which had tiny feathered nestlings inside, and then walked back home. It was about half-past two, and the other members of the Secret Seven were waiting in the summer-house.

They were very downcast at Peter's news. 'Well, we were none of us successful in our scarecrow-hunt this morning,' said Jack, 'and no wonder, if the loot had been buried by *your* scarecrow, Peter. What bad luck! If only we'd been able to dig by your scarecrow last night, perhaps we'd have got the hidden goods before Albert.'

'What shall we do now?' asked Pam. 'Everything seems dull suddenly, now that we've not got our cave any more, and the adventure has faded away.'

'I'm going up to the cave,' said Jack, standing up. 'I think I left my torch there, high up on a ledge. I hope Albert hasn't taken it! It's rather a nice one, and I'd like to get it if it's still there.'

'Right, we'll all come, just for the walk,' said Peter. 'We could take spades and dig in the old quarry, the sand is moist in parts, and you can model quite well with it. Let's do that.'

So they took four spades from the shed and three trowels, and off they went to the quarry. Jack went up to the cave and then stopped short in surprise.

Someone was there! He could hear excited voices. Then he frowned. He knew *one* voice – it was Susie's! Bother her, now she would mess about round them, and make silly re-marks. Who was with her? It sounded like Jeff. What cheek to come to the cave! Just like Susie!

He went into the cave, still frowning. Susie and Jeff were right at the back, scrabbling about. Whatever were they doing?

'Susie!' he called sharply. 'What are you doing here?'

Susie turned round and then came quickly over to her brother. 'Jack! I *am* glad you've come. Something peculiar has happened!'

'What?' asked Jack impatiently. 'I think it's pretty peculiar that you and Jeff should come to *our* cave, even though we've left it.'

'Don't be cross, Jack. I really am glad you've come,' said Susie. 'Listen. Jeff and I came here, and we thought it was a lovely place. We made deep holes for ourselves. Mine's over there, look, and Jeff's is opposite, by the rocky wall. We thought perhaps you others might be coming, so we practically *covered* ourselves with sand, just left our noses out to breathe, and we waited for you so that we could give loud yells and leap out at you when you came in thinking nobody was here . . .'

Jack gave a snort. 'Is that all you've got to tell me? *Not* very interesting.'

'Oh, *do* listen, Jack,' said Susie. 'Well, we lay like mice, only our noses out, waiting for you to come in at the front entrance there, and then somebody came out from the *back* of the cave, and trod heavily on poor Jeff and went out of the entrance!'

'And yet we *know* the cave was empty when we came in,' said Jeff. 'We looked to make sure. But there's nowhere for anyone to hide or to come from, so who was this person, and how did he get here?'

Jack was now listening intently. This was news! He turned to the entrance of the cave and yelled loudly: 'PETER! JANET! EVERY-BODY! COME HERE QUICKLY! QUICKLY, I SAY!'

[14]

What an excitement!

Peter, Janet, and all the others threw down their spades and trowels and raced to the cave at top speed. 'What is it?' cried Peter.

Then he saw Susie and Jeff and stopped. 'Clear out,' he cried. 'This is our cave, not yours.'

'Wait, Peter,' said Jack. 'Susie's just told me something strange.' He told the others what Susie had said, how she and Jeff had buried themselves all but their noses in the empty cave, and then someone had come from the back and walked out!

'So there *is* some way into this cave from the back,' he said. 'I know we've looked and looked, but there *must* be! Susie, did you hear anything at all before this man walked out of the cave?'

'Yes,' said Susie. 'I heard a kind of thud – so did Jeff.'

'As if someone had leapt down to the sandy floor,' said Jeff. 'Like this!' He jumped into the air and came down, making a soft thud.

'Then the way in from the back must be from somewhere up near the roof,' said Peter. 'Anyone got a torch?'

'Here's mine,' said Jack. 'I found it on the ledge where I'd left it.'

Peter took it. 'Come on,' he said. 'We're jolly well going to solve this mystery. Wait though – Colin, keep guard at the front of the cave, in case that man comes back. Take a good look at him if he does.'

'Right,' said Colin, and limped to the front of the cave, though he would dearly have liked to be with the others.

There was quite a crowd at the back of the

cave. Peter shone his torch on to the roof there. It was fairly high. He saw a rocky ledge jutting out and thought he would climb up to it. 'Give me a hand,' he said to Jack. 'Hold the torch for a minute, Janet.'

He was soon up on the ledge, and then shone the torch on to the roof again. He gave a sudden exclamation.

'What is it?' shouted everyone, almost dancing with excitement.

'There's a round hole here. You can't see it from where you are,' said Peter. 'And there's a rope-end hanging down. I can just reach it.'

The others craned their necks to see what Peter saw, but they couldn't. The hole was hidden by a jutting-out piece of rock, and it was only because Peter was high up on the ledge that he could see it at all. He shone his torch on the thick rope-end. It was well within his reach from the ledge on which he stood.

He stuffed the torch into his pocket. 'I can

get hold of the rope,' he called down, 'and I think I can pull myself up by it. I'll try anyway.'

He caught the rope in both hands, and then by means of treading on first one narrow ledge of rock and then another, he managed to get right into the hole. He let go of the ledges with his feet and swung on the rope with his hands. He climbed up it as he did at gym, and came to a broad ledge, where he rested for a moment or two.

Then he stood on the ledge, putting his head up through the hole that still went upwards, and found that he was looking out of the hole into another cave above! He shone his torch around.

He gave a yell to the others down below, but to them his voice sounded curiously muffled and hollow. They were quite startled to hear it.

'Hey! There's another cave here, a much smaller one! And some of our food's here, and all our cushions, and books and magazines! And there's a bag too, a small mailbag that looks full of something!'

'What? What do you say?' yelled the others, almost overcome with excitement at all this shouting, and not being able to make out a word.

'PETER! What have you found?' cried Janet.

Peter came down from the rope, found the ledge he needed to climb down from, and leapt to the ground. He pushed the others away as they crowded round him, and went to get some air at the front of the cave.

'Tell us! What did you find?' said Jack. 'We heard you yelling.'

'There's a cave up there with all our things in it. That man Albert used the cushions to lie on, because the floor is of hard rock, not soft sand,' said Peter. '*And* there's a bag, a mail-bag, I think. Probably full of registered envelopes! Goodness knows how long it was buried beneath our scarecrow.'

'Well, that's a find!' said Janet, her eyes shining. 'Now we know how our mysterious visitor got into the cave without passing through the front entrance, when he wanted to steal our things. How thrilled he must have been to find food and cushions and books!'

'Now listen,' said Peter. 'He may come back at any minute, but he won't dare to come into the cave while people are there. I'm going to tell Dad, and he'll phone the police. You stay here, all of you, till I come back, then Albert won't be able to remove the stolen mailbag! I'll leave Scamper with you too.'

'Right,' said Jack, taking charge. 'We'll make a good bit of noise too, shall we, to scare him off if he comes! Well done finding that cave above, Peter. You *are* clever!'

'Well, *I* really put you on to it,' said Susie. 'Gosh, I was glad to see you, Jack.'

'You were wrong to come to our cave, but

for once in a way you were right to tell me what you'd seen,' said Jack sternly. 'Now, if you want to stay with us, behave yourself, Susie. Do you hear?'

'Yes, teacher,' said Susie demurely. 'I'll be a good, good girl. I'll—'

'Be quiet,' said Jack, 'or out you both go, you and Jeff!'

Susie looked at Jack's face and was suddenly quiet. They all were for a minute or two, thinking over the startling happenings of the last few minutes. Then they remembered that Peter wanted them to make a noise, so that Albert would not come to the cave to try to get that mailbag! They began to talk and laugh.

Peter ran at top speed to find his father. 'Dad!' he called, seeing him by the barn. 'Hey, DAD! Quick, I want you!'

[15]

A wonderful finish!

Peter's father could not make head or tail of the boy's breathless story at first. But at last he made out enough to call his wife.

'Will you telephone to the police and tell them to come at once, and go to the cave in the quarry?' he called. 'I'm off there with Peter. Tell you what's up when I get back!'

He went off with the excited Peter. Soon they were at the cave, where the others, talking loudly, were waiting anxiously. The green curtain was tied back now, and Peter's father gazed into the cave.

'I'd forgotten this old cave,' he said. 'I used to love it when I was a boy. Do you really mean to say there's a cave *above* it, Peter? I never knew that, and yet I played here heaps of times.'

'So did we,' said Janet. 'Come and see where the hole is that leads into the cave above.'

'We had this cave for our Secret Seven meetings,' explained Peter, 'and we *couldn't* make out who took our things, or why. We didn't guess someone was in hiding in a cave above us! There's a mailbag up there, Dad. Do you think the man stole it?'

'Probably. You'd better shin up and get it when the police come,' said Peter's father. 'I wonder how long it's been hidden there? Quite a long time, maybe.'

'No, only since last night,' said Peter. 'It was buried beside that scarecrow in the oat-field, Dad!'

'So *that's* why you were so interested in scarecrows all of a sudden,' said his father. 'I wonder if your mother has telephoned the police yet. Run back and see if they're coming, Peter.'

Peter set off through the quarry with Scamper at his heels, but halfway through

Scamper left him and ran behind a hummock, barking madly. Peter followed him. He saw a curious mound in the sand, which, as Scamper leapt on it, put out hands and feet – and head!

'Call him off!' said a voice. 'Call him off!'

'Who are you?' demanded Peter, catching Scamper by the collar. 'Hey, *I* know who you are, you're Albert, aren't you? Waiting till we're all gone so that you can fetch that stolen mailbag and empty it! You meant to leave the bag up in that cave, stuff your pockets with the contents, and slip away free! You'll—'

'Now, now,' said a deep voice, 'what's all this, and who is this fellow lying in the sand? Ah, surely it's Albert Tanner! We've been looking for you, Albert, ever since that last mail robbery.'

It was the big Inspector of Police! Behind him was a stolid village constable, looking as if this kind of thing was very ordinary indeed.

The Inspector turned to Peter and beamed at him. 'Hello, Peter! I knew as soon as your mother phoned that you were caught up into one of your adventures. Is Albert here anything to do with it?'

'Yes,' said Peter. 'Look, my father's over there, by the cave. He's waiting for you.'

'Bring Albert along,' said the Inspector to his policeman, and Albert was duly brought along to the cave. As soon as Peter's father saw him, he gave an exclamation.

'Why! It's Albert Tanner! I thought I told you never to show your face in this district again, Albert!'

'You know him, sir, do you?' said the Inspector, getting out a big notebook.

'I should think I do!' said Peter's father. 'He was brought up here on this land, in a cottage not far off, and worked for me for a few years. But he was so dishonest I had to dismiss him.'

'That's how he knew this cave then!' said

Peter. '*And* the one above. He must have explored like we did.'

Albert didn't say a word. He stood there, sullen and angry. The Inspector threw a glance at him. Then he turned to Peter's father.

'This man and another did a mailbag robbery,' he said. 'The other man hid the bag somewhere, meaning to get it when the commotion about it died down. He worked on this farm once too, sir – his name's Ted Yorks.'

'Ted Yorks! Yes, he was here for years,' said Peter's father. 'He was a bad lot too, but a fine hedger and ditcher, which is why I kept him so long.'

'Well, as I said, these two planned this robbery,' said the Inspector, 'and the mail-bag was hidden, ready to be found and the contents shared between the two of them in due course. But Ted got caught and put into prison, where he is still.'

'But he managed to get a note out of prison

to Albert, to tell him how to find out where he had hidden the bag!' cried Peter. 'I see it all now! Albert came to this cave to hide till he heard from Ted, because he knew the police here were still looking for him, and he didn't dare to show his face—'

'And when he got Ted's note, he went to meet that man Jim, the one on the seat by the post office, and learnt that he had to look by the scarecrow!' said Jack. 'I heard Jim say "The Scarecrow. That's where it is." And of course, Albert knew it was *our* scarecrow!'

'These kids know all about you, you see, Albert,' said the Inspector, looking at the surly man. 'Where did you put that mailbag after you'd dug it up, Albert?'

'I'm not saying anything,' said Albert, 'except that I don't know anything about any mailbag, and it's no use asking me.'

'I'll get the mailbag, shall I?' said Peter, much to the Inspector's surprise. He looked at Peter, quite astounded.

'The mailbag? Don't tell me you know where *that* is?' he said. 'Right, get it.'

So off went Peter to the back of the cave, shinned up the wall, caught hold of the rope, and disappeared. Then a voice came down the hole.

'Stand by, everyone! Mailbag on the way!' There was a heavy thud on the soft sand, and there was the mailbag! Its fall had broken it open, and registered envelopes and packets came tumbling out.

'Whew!' said the Inspector, amazed. 'This is magic! Hey, Peter, any more mailbags to come?'

Peter came down the hole, laughing. 'No. That's the only one. Is it the stolen one?'

'Yes,' said the Inspector. 'Well, I'm afraid Albert won't be able to steal any more mail-bags for a long, long time. Take him away, Constable!'

Albert was marched away, still sullen and silent. 'Come in and have a word with my wife, Inspector,' said Peter's father. 'She must be longing to know what all this excitement's about. Peter, here's some money. Take all the Secret Seven out and give them a thumping good tea, ice-creams and all. You've done well, my boy!'

He went off with the Inspector, who waved a cheery hand to them. Peter turned to the others, beaming. He waved the money at them.

'Look at that! We'll have a feast. Come on!'

Susie and Jeff went out of the cave with the others. Jack gave his sister a little push.

'You're not coming with *us*, Susie. We're the Secret Seven, and you don't belong. You go home.'

'Oh,' said Janet, seeing Susie's downcast face, 'couldn't she come just for once? I mean, she did tell you about Albert coming out of the back of the cave when she and Jeff were there, Jack, and it was because of that

that we managed to find the other cave at last. *Couldn't* she come?'

'No. We're the Secret Seven,' said Jack, 'and Susie would only laugh and sneer at us all the time, like she always does. And Jeff too. No.'

'I won't! I think you're wonderful!' said Susie. 'Let me come. Just this once, Jack. I DO want to hear all about this exciting adventure.'

'You can come, Susie,' said Peter, taking command. '*And* Jeff too. Just this once. It's a story worth telling, I promise you. It will take us at least four ice-creams each before the tale is told. It's a jolly good adventure, you'll have to admit that, Susie!'

It was, and Susie's going to say so, too, when she's heard it. Good old Secret Seven – they always get there in the end, don't they?

THREE CHEERS, SECRET SEVEN

[1]

No meeting after all!

'I don't see much sense in calling a Secret Seven meeting,' said Janet to Peter. 'There's really nothing to discuss – no adventure or mystery anywhere – and I did want to finish reading my book.'

'We haven't had a meeting for three weeks,' said Peter. 'And if you've got something better to do than to belong to the Secret Seven and attend the meetings, well, do it! We can easily get somebody instead of you.'

'Peter! Don't be so cross!' said Janet, quite horrified at the thought of not being a Secret Seven member. 'Of *course* I want to belong. But it's only *really* exciting when something is happening. Or if we've got plenty to eat and drink.'

'Well, if the others bring what they promised we should have quite a nice feast,' said Peter. 'Do help me to tidy the shed ready for the others, Janet – you just sit there and do nothing!'

The two of them and Scamper were down at the meeting-shed getting ready for the other five. On the door were the big letters, SS, and Scamper, the golden spaniel, sat outside as if guarding the shed. It was quite an ordinary shed in the usual way, but it seemed very important to Scamper when the Secret Seven held a meeting there.

'Here comes someone,' said Peter, as Scamper gave a small bark of welcome.

'Rat-tat!' There came a sharp knock on the closed door of the shed.

'Password!' called Peter. 'And don't yell it, please!'

'Lollipops!' said a voice, with a little giggle at the end.

'That's Pam,' said Janet. 'Come in, friend!'

Pam came in, carrying a small bag. 'Hallo!' she said. 'Am I the first? I've brought some biscuits – but there aren't many, I'm afraid.'

'Wuff-wuff!' said Scamper, from outside, and more footsteps could be heard.

'Lollipops!' said a low voice. And then another voice said, 'Peppermints!' and laughed.

Peter went to the door at once. George and Colin were there. 'Come in, George,' said Peter. 'Stay out, Colin; you didn't know the password.'

'Oh, come on! That was only a joke!' said Colin, hastily. 'Honestly it was, Lollipops is such a silly password – I just improved on it by saying "peppermints". Ask George if I didn't *really* know the password. I told him it coming along. Didn't I, George?'

'Yes – he does know the password really, Peter,' said George. 'Let him in.'

'Well, I will *this* time,' said Peter. 'Hallo, here comes Barbara – and Jack. But who's that waiting about over there?'

'It's *Susie*!' said Janet. 'That horrid sister of Jack's. I bet she'll try to come to the meeting.'

'Password, Barbara,' said Peter. Barbara and Jack both remembered it and went into the shed. Peter watched Susie for a few moments, but she didn't come any nearer, so he went in and shut the door of the shed. He left Scamper on guard outside.

'On guard!' he said, and Scamper sat down and waited, knowing perfectly well that he must bark if anyone came near. He watched Susie intently. If she dared to come one step nearer he would bark in his very fiercest voice!

Peter turned on Jack as soon as the shed-door closed. 'Whatever do you want to bring that awful sister of yours here for?' he demanded. 'You know how often she's upset our meetings, and got to know our passwords!'

'Well, she's promised not to come *near* our shed,' said Jack. 'And though I agree she's an awful nuisance, she does keep her word, you know. She won't disturb us, really she won't.'

'But why did you want to bring her at *all*?' said Peter. 'I don't trust her one bit. I bet she wants to play some silly trick on us.'

'She doesn't. But I'll tell you why I *had* to bring her,' said Jack. 'An American cousin of ours has sent her an aeroplane, and she can't fly it by herself. I'm longing to have a go at it. So we're going to fly it after the meeting somewhere. We've left it under your hedge till the meeting is over.'

'An aeroplane? What sort?' said George, eagerly.

'A *fantastic* one,' said Jack. 'As big as

this!' and he held his arms out wide. 'And it's got some kind of clockwork to wind up the elastic bands that help it to fly. I tell you, it's super!'

'Fancy sending an aeroplane to *Susie*!' said Peter, amazed. 'Why didn't your cousin send it to you, Jack?'

'Well, we were each asked what we wanted,' said Jack. 'I chose a cowboy outfit – it's fine – and Susie chose an aeroplane. Just like Susie to choose something *I* want when it comes. It's miles nicer than my cowboy-suit.'

'Would Susie let us come and see you fly it?' asked George.

Jack looked doubtful. 'I don't know. She's always rather cross about the Secret Seven, you know, because we keep her out of it.'

'I tell you what!' said Peter, quite changing his mind about Susie, now that she owned such a wonderful aeroplane. 'Let's *not* make this a Secret Seven meeting. Let's take our food into the garden somewhere, and tell Susie she can join us – if she'll let us help with the aeroplane.'

'Right,' said Jack. 'I'll ask her,' and out he went to speak to Susie.

He came back at once. 'Yes! She says she'll join our feast, and we'll go and fly the plane afterwards,' he said, putting his head in at the shed. 'Come on, bring out the food!'

So out they all went, and Susie joined them, grinning all over her freckled face.

'Hallo!' she said cheekily. 'We're not the Secret Seven this morning – we're the Exciting Eight!'

[2]

The beautiful aeroplane

Peter didn't like Susie's remark that they were not the Secret Seven at the moment, but the Exciting Eight. However, it wouldn't do to make her cross by snapping at her just when they all wanted a favour from her.

'Where's this super plane?' he asked.

'Where's this super food?' said Susie at once. 'We'll have that first before we fly the plane.'

'All right, all right. We meant to, anyhow,' said Peter. 'Where shall we have it? Over there under that tree?'

'No. I tell you what we'll do,' said Jack. 'Susie and I were going to fly the plane in the big field behind our house, so what about taking the food there and sitting on the grass? It's a nice field.'

'Yes. Good idea,' said Peter, and the others agreed. 'Come on, Scamper, walk-ie-walk!'

'Wuff!' said Scamper, pleased, and acted like his name, scampering off at top speed to the front gate. He stopped and gazed suspiciously at something hidden under the hedge, and then barked again.

'It's all right, Scamper, it's only my aeroplane,' said Susie, proudly. The Seven stopped to admire it. It stood there under the hedge, the biggest toy aeroplane they had ever seen, gleaming silver-bright in the sun.

All the children thought the same thing. Fancy that beautiful plane belonging to *Susie*. What a dreadful waste! But none of them said that, knowing perfectly well that if they did, the annoying Susie would pick up the plane and march off with it all by herself.

'Well, what do you think of it?' asked Susie. 'Better than a silly cowboy-suit, isn't it?'

Jack went red and glared at his sister. 'If I'd known that *this* was the kind of aeroplane our American cousin was going to send—' he began, angrily, but Peter stopped him.

'Don't go up in smoke, Jack,' he said, anxious to keep the peace. 'I bet your suit is super. But gosh, WHAT an aeroplane! It's even got retractable landing wheels, look!'

'Yes,' said Susie, proudly. 'In the leaflet about the plane, it says that the wheels go up into the body as soon as the plane starts flying, and are put out again automatically when it lands. I bet no one in the whole country has a model aeroplane that does that.'

The Secret Seven felt sure she was right.

Susie picked up the beautiful plane and went out of the front gate.

'*I'll* carry it for you,' said Peter. 'I'm sure it's too heavy for you!'

Susie laughed in her usual annoying way. 'What you *really* mean is that you're longing to carry it yourself so that everyone we meet will think it's *yours* and envy you!' she said. 'Ha, you're going red! *I* know you boys. But the plane is *mine* and *I'm* doing the carrying, thank you.'

Nobody said any more. What a pity Jack had such a clever sister. You could never get the better of Susie! She always had a smart answer ready. The little procession set out down the road, Susie first with the plane, then the others straggling behind and Scamper last of all, sniffing into all the corners as usual.

They came to Jack's house, went in at the side gate, and down to the bottom of the garden at the back. There they had to climb over a fence to get into the vast field that lay beyond.

'Food first,' said Susie, when they were all over, and Scamper had been lifted safely down to the ground.

'What food have *you* brought?' said Pam, who was beginning to feel annoyed with Susie.

'None. *I've* brought the aeroplane,' said Susie. 'I hope *you* haven't brought the miserable biscuits you bring to school to eat at break!'

'Shut up, Susie,' said Jack, uncomfortably. 'We've got a jolly good feast. You can have a very fair share, and remember that it doesn't cost you anything to be polite.'

The feast was certainly quite good. There were the biscuits, of course, some rock buns, pieces of gingerbread, an enormous bar of nut chocolate, jam-tarts, two bottles of lemonade, and a bag of toffees.

'Give Scamper a toffee,' said George. 'That will keep him quiet for ages.'

But Scamper wanted a bit of everything, and got it too. He had only to lie down by any of the Seven and look at them beseechingly out of his great brown eyes to get anything he wanted! Even Susie gave him a titbit and patted him.

'Now we'll fly the plane,' she said, when every crumb had been finished, and every drop of lemonade had been drunk. At once everyone stood up, excited. Jack took up the leaflet about the plane and studied it, while the other three boys tried to look over his shoulder.

'It seems easy enough,' said Jack.

'All I want is for you to show me what to do the *first* time and I'll know forever afterwards,' said Susie. 'Now, what happens?'

'Well, you turn this, that's to make sure the wheels go back as soon as the plane is in the air,' said Jack. 'And you press this, look,

Susie. And you wind up the key here – that's the mechanism that winds the elastic bands up tightly so that they give the plane the energy to fly, and—'

'I don't want all those explanations,' said Susie, impatiently. 'I just want to know how to *fly* the plane.'

Jack said no more, but pressed this and that, and wound the little key till it would wind no more. Then he held the beautiful plane high above his head and pressed a little button at the back.

'Fly!' he shouted, and threw the plane forward. It rose high into the air at once, with a loud, humming noise. It circled round beautifully while the children watched it in delight. Then it rose high into the air and flew off across the field to the other side, for all the world like a real plane.

'It will turn and circle back to us,' said Jack. 'That's what the booklet said.'

But it didn't! It kept straight on, flew over

a high wall at the other side of the field, and disappeared completely!

'Oh no!' said Jack, horrified, 'It hasn't come back. *Now* what are we to do?'

[3]

Where is the aeroplane?

'It's gone!' said Susie, looking quite heart-broken. 'My beautiful aeroplane! Oh, I wouldn't have let you fly it, Jack, if I'd thought you'd lose it on its very first flight. It will be smashed to pieces!'

'*I* didn't know it would do that!' said Jack. 'Whoever saw a model plane fly like that before? I never guessed it would be able to fly right across this big field. Oh, Susie, I'm awfully sorry, really I am.'

'Who lives in that place?' asked Peter, looking towards the high wall. 'Is there a house there?'

'Yes. It's called Bartlett Lodge, and it's a very big house,' said Jack. 'It's been shut up for ages, because the owners left to go abroad.'

'Oh, well, we could easily go and get the plane then,' said George. 'No one will shout at us or chase us if we look for it.'

'There's a gardener there,' said Jack, doubtfully. 'He's not very nice. When Susie and I lost our ball over there he wouldn't even let us climb over the wall to get it, though *he* couldn't find it. So we lost it.'

'*I'm* not going over,' said Barbara. 'I'd be scared. I don't like cross gardeners.'

'No one has to go if they don't want to,' said Peter firmly. 'Perhaps only four of us should go anyway. Eight is too many to make a quick getaway if necessary. We'll climb up to the top of the wall and see if the gardener's there. If he is, we'll be awfully polite, and apologetic, and ask if he's seen our plane. If he's *not* there, we'll go over and hunt.'

'Hadn't you better ask permission before you do that?' said Janet.

'Who from?' said Jack. 'There's nobody in the house to ask. Come on – we'll see what we can do.'

All the eight, and Scamper too, went across the field to the high wall. 'How are you going to climb that?' said Barbara. 'It's terribly high.'

'We'll shove each other up,' said Jack. 'I'll go first and have a look from the top of the wall to see if the gardener is anywhere about.'

George and Peter pushed him up, and at last he was on the top of the wall. He looked down into the overgrown shrubbery on the other side. Through a gap he could spy an unmown lawn, but there was no gardener to be seen. He put his hands to his mouth and shouted.

'Hey! Anybody there?' He listened, but there was no answer. Jack called again. 'Can I come over the wall and look for our aeroplane, please?'

Then a voice suddenly shouted back.

'Who's that? Where are you?'

'Here, on the top of the wall!' yelled Jack. He turned and looked down at the others. 'I can see the man. He's coming. Perhaps he's got the plane.'

A man came quickly through the gap in the trees. He was thick-set, and broad-shouldered, and had a ruddy, surly face, with screwed-up eyes. In his hand was a spade.

'Now then, what are you doing on that wall?' he said, threateningly. 'You get off. This here is private property and well you know it! Do you know what I do to children who come in here? I chase them with a spade!'

'We don't want to come in,' said Jack, rather alarmed. 'We just wanted to know if you've seen our aeroplane. It flew right over the—'

'No. I've not seen *any* aeroplane, or *any*

ball, or *any* kite, and what's more if I find one it can stay here,' said the surly man. 'You've got a big enough field back there to play in without throwing things over here. If I find a plane I shall put it on my bonfire.'

'Oh, *no*!' said Jack, in horror. 'It's a very valuable plane, a real beauty. Oh please, *do* let me come down and look for it, it belongs to my sister, and I—'

'If it belonged to the Queen of England I'd not let you come in here,' said the man. 'Understand? I've got my orders, see? I'm in charge of this place while it's empty, and I'm not having any boys coming in here to steal the fruit, or—'

'I'm not a thief!' said Jack, indignantly. 'I just wanted our plane. I'll tell my father, and *he'll* come and get it for me.'

'*That* he won't,' said the surly gardener. 'Now you clear off that wall this minute, or I'll tip you off!' He held up his spade as if he meant what he said. Jack didn't want to be shovelled off like a sack of potatoes, and leapt down very hastily into the field.

'What a beast!' said Peter, to poor Jack, as the boy sprawled heavily on the grass, for it was a high jump down from the wall.

'YOU SEND ME BACK MY AEROPLANE!' suddenly shouted Susie, stamping her foot on the grass, tears in her eyes at the thought of losing the aeroplane on its very first flight. But there was no answer at all from over the wall.

'Oh, Susie, I'm so sorry,' said Jack, getting up. 'Listen, I'll go and get the plane for you, really I will, as soon as that horrible man has gone off for his dinner. I expect he goes at about twelve o'clock.'

Everyone crowded round Susie, feeling really upset about the lovely plane. 'Didn't you even *see* it anywhere?' asked Susie, in a fierce voice, turning to Jack. He shook his head dolefully.

'Listen,' said Peter, taking command

again. 'Two of us will go and watch at the front gates of that house, and then, as soon as we see that horrible gardener going off for his midday dinner, we'll know it's safe to slip over the wall and hunt for the plane. We won't go in at the front gates in case anyone sees us and tells the gardener.'

'Good idea,' said Jack, cheering up. 'You and I will go, Peter. What's the time? Gosh, it's almost twelve now! Come on, let's sprint down that little lane to the road that the house faces on. Hurry up!'

Jack and Peter set off down a narrow little lane that led from the field to the road on which the big house faced. They turned to the left in the road and came to the big gate that led into the drive of Bartlett Lodge. There was a second gate farther on that also led into the drive.

'You watch that gate, I'll watch this one,' said Peter. 'But hide behind a tree or something. You don't want that gardener to see you. He's already seen you up on the wall, and he may recognise you and chase you.'

'Don't worry, I won't let him spot me, and if he does, I bet I can run faster than he does!' said Jack, and set off towards the second gate.

There was a workmen's shed a little farther down the road, and he decided to hide behind that. So he posted himself there. Peter went across the road and hid behind a bush that most conveniently grew there. Now, would that tiresome man soon come out?

They had waited about ten minutes when they saw someone coming out of the gate nearest Peter. Jack signalled to Peter, and he nodded back. It was the gardener, no doubt about that. Jack recognised the burly figure at once, and drew back behind the shed.

The man set off down the road and turned the corner. Jack whistled to Peter, and the two ran to the little lane together, to go and tell the others that the gardener had gone.

They were in the field, playing with a ball, waiting impatiently for the boys to come back. Susie was still upset about her plane, and had been making quite a lot of rude remarks about the Secret Seven. They were getting rather tired of her!

'Here are the boys!' said Janet, as they appeared in the field. 'Any news, Peter?'

'Yes. That man's gone to his dinner, as we hoped,' said Peter. 'Now we can try and get Susie's plane. We'll go over the wall as before.'

'I'm coming too,' said Susie, unexpectedly.

'You are *not*,' said Jack at once.

'Well, it's my plane, isn't it?' said the irritating Susie. 'I've got every right to go and look for it. I'm coming too.'

'YOU ARE NOT!' said Peter, in the voice that all the rest of the Secret Seven knew well, and didn't dream of disobeying. But Susie wasn't going to take orders from Peter.

'I shall do as I like,' she said, defiantly. 'I shall climb the wall too.'

'Well, I don't know how,' said Peter, 'because I shall certainly forbid anyone to give you a shove up.'

He and Jack were quickly hoisted up to the top of the wall by George and Colin. Susie stood by, looking sulky. She turned to the two boys near her. 'Now give *me* a shove,' she said.

'Nothing doing,' said Colin, cheerfully. 'Peter's our chief, as you jolly well know, and he's given his orders. Don't be an idiot, Susie.'

'I'll climb up by myself then,' said Susie, and she very nearly did, using every little hole and crevice for her feet and fingers! The others watched her angrily – but to their delight she could not reach the top, and fell down when she was half-way up.

'Have you hurt yourself?' asked Janet, anxiously. But Susie refused to cry or to say she was hurt. She made a rude face at Janet and stood up, brushing her skirt with her hand. She walked a little way away from the others, and leaned against the wall, whistling as if she didn't care tuppence for any of the Secret Seven.

The boys had now disappeared from the top of the wall. There was a most convenient tree that leaned towards the wall just there, and one by one the boys gave the little leap towards it that enabled them to catch hold of a branch and then swing themselves neatly to the ground.

They stood there, all looking cautiously towards the house, through the gap in the shrubbery. No one was to be seen, of course, and as the house was not over-looked by any other, they felt that they could go safely forward and hunt for Susie's aeroplane.

'I hope it's not smashed to bits,' said Jack to Peter, as they made their way through the trees and bushes towards the great untidy lawn. 'If it is I'll never hear the last of it from Susie. She never forgets a thing like that!'

They began to hunt for the aeroplane. First they searched the beds round the lawn, but no plane was there, only masses of weeds that made the boys wonder what the gardener did for his wages! They hunted in the bushes, they looked up into the trees, wondering if the plane had caught in some high branch.

'This is maddening!' said Jack, at last. 'Not a *sign* of the plane! Do you suppose that gardener found it and hid it away?'

'I shouldn't be surprised!' said Peter. 'He's surly enough for anything!'

They were now fairly near the great house. It looked very forbidding, for all the curtains were drawn straight across the windows. And then Peter suddenly saw the aeroplane.

It had landed neatly on a little balcony on the second floor of the house, and there it was, balanced on the broad stone ledge.

'Look, there it is!' said Peter, pointing. 'And if we climb this tree that goes right up to the balcony we can easily get it. It's not smashed. It looks perfectly all right!'

'You go up, and I'll keep watch down here,' said Jack. 'I don't know why, but I suddenly feel nervous. I hope that gardener hasn't come back!'

[4]

Something rather strange

Peter began to climb the tree. It was quite easy and safe. Jack stood at the bottom, watching him, looking all round now and again in case that bad-tempered gardener came back!

It didn't take Peter long to get up as far as the second-floor balcony. He climbed over it, and examined the aeroplane. Was it broken in any way?

Most miraculously it seemed to be perfectly all right, nothing bent or broken at all. It had, in fact, made a perfect landing in a very difficult place! Peter called down to Jack.

'Hey! The plane's not damaged at all. Isn't that a bit of luck? I'm wondering what is the best way to get it down. I can't very well climb down the tree with it because I need both my hands.'

'Got a piece of string?' called back Jack. 'If you have, you could tie one end to the tail of the plane, and let it down carefully to me.'

'Oh, yes, of course! Good idea!' said Peter. He always carried string about with him, of course, as did all the Secret Seven; you never knew when it might come in useful in any sudden adventure, and, in the opinion of the Secret Seven, adventures were nearly always sudden!

Peter took the string out of his pocket and undid it. Yes, it would just about reach down to Jack. He began to tie one end to the tail of the plane, marvelling at the beautiful workmanship in it as he did so. No wonder Susie was proud of such a model. But oh, what a *waste* for it to belong to her!

He carefully let the plane down to Jack, who stood with his hands outstretched, waiting to receive it, most thankful that it wasn't damaged. Now perhaps Susie would hold her tongue!

'I've got it! Thanks awfully, Peter!' he called up. 'Come on down, and we'll take it back to Susie.'

Peter glanced round the balcony to make sure that he was leaving nothing behind. The curtains of the balcony room were drawn across, just as they were in all the rooms of the house – but they did not quite meet in the middle. And then just as Peter was turning away to climb over to the tree, something caught his eye. Something red and glowing, shining between the cracks of the curtains just where they did not meet.

He stopped, astonished. Why, that looked like a light, or a fire burning in the balcony room! But it couldn't be – the house was shut up and empty!

Gosh, I hope a fire hasn't started up somehow, thought Peter, alarmed. I'd better peep through the window and see. Perhaps I can open the balcony window.

He went to the window and peered through the crack of the curtains. Yes, he was right, there *was* a fire glowing in the room! But wait a minute – it was a gas-fire, surely?

He pressed his face against the glass of the window, and, when his eyes became used to the dimness of the curtained room, he could see quite clearly that a gas-fire was burning brightly in the fireplace. What a very extraordinary thing!

He tried the window to see if he could open it, but it was fastened inside. Gosh, had the people left that fire on when they went away? What a terrible waste of gas! It certainly ought to be turned off.

He was just peering to see what else he

could spy between the curtains when he heard Jack's voice.

'Peter! What on earth are you doing? Do come down!'

'I'm just—' began Peter, when Jack called again, suddenly sounding scared.

'Peter! I can hear someone whistling. I think it's that gardener coming back. HUR-RY UP!'

Peter had a shock. Gosh, it would never do to get caught by that awful man! He shot over the balcony at once, and was climbing down the tree before Jack could call again!

'Come on,' said Jack, urgently. 'What-ever made you so long? I'm sure it's that gardener about somewhere!'

But there was no sign of the man, much to Peter's relief. It must have been someone else whistling. He and Jack tore down the garden to the bottom, and stopped to get their breath in the shrubbery by the wall.

'Listen, Jack,' panted Peter. 'I saw something rather odd in that balcony room. I think we'll call a meeting about it. So can you make Susie go off with her plane, and then we'll be able to plan a meeting this afternoon?'

'Oooh, what did you see? What's up?' said Jack, at once.

'No time to talk about it now,' said Peter, looking at his watch. 'Anyway, I'd rather tell it to everybody at a meeting. Come on, let's shin up this tree and get over the wall. I'll hold the plane and hand it to you when you're at the top.'

He called over the wall. 'Hey, are you there, Colin and George?'

'Yes! Have you found the plane?' called the two boys on the other side.

'Yes. We're coming over. Stand by to help,' said Peter.

He waited till Jack had climbed the tree and was sitting on the wall, and then handed him the precious plane, which Jack then handed down carefully to Colin. There was the sound of delighted voices at once!

Then up went Peter and was soon on the wall grinning down at the others. He saw Susie proudly holding her plane again, smiling all over her face.

'Better take it home straightaway, Susie,' said Jack, remembering that he had to get rid of his sister somehow.

'I'm jolly well *going* to,' said Susie. 'I'm not letting the Secret Seven fly it again!' And off she went, head in the air!

'Listen, Secret Seven,' said Peter, urgently. 'Meet this afternoon at half-past two. I've got something to tell you all. Not a word to Susie, though!'

'Right!' said everyone, excited, and Scamper barked too. Ah, was something going to happen at last?

[5]

A *proper meeting*

The Secret Seven met very punctually indeed that afternoon, for they were all very anxious to know why Peter had called such a sudden meeting. Jack arrived first, ten minutes early and quite out of breath.

'Lollipops!' he panted, and was let into the shed at once. 'I've given Susie the slip – I *hope*!' he said. 'She wanted me to go fishing in the ponds with her this afternoon, and I had an awful bother trying to put her off. I think she half suspects there's another meeting on. I ran like a hare as soon as I could give her the slip!'

'Bother Susie!' said Peter. 'We'll put old Scamper on guard again outside the door. And, by the way, Jack, there's no food for the meeting to have this afternoon, because we ate it all this morning, and my mother won't let me have another lot.'

'Same here,' said Jack. 'Listen, here are the others. Goodness, aren't we nice and early! It's only twenty-five past two.'

'Wuff-wuff!' said Scamper, as the usual knock came at the door of the shed, and the password was muttered by the other four members.

'Pass, friends!' called Peter, and in they all came, with Scamper at their heels. He always knew when the whole seven were there!

'Sorry, Scamper, old thing, but I want you to keep guard outside,' said Peter, and gave him a gentle push. 'Bark if Susie so much as puts her nose in at the front gate!'

Scamper put his tail down mournfully, and went to sit outside. He sensed that there was excitement about and he wanted to share it. Still Peter was the chief, and Scamper, like the others, obeyed him at once.

They were soon all sitting round on boxes and flowerpots, their eyes fixed expectantly on Peter.

'What's this sudden meeting for?' asked Colin. 'Is something up?'

'I don't know. But I thought I'd tell you and we'd discuss it,' said Peter. 'There may be absolutely nothing in it – but if there is, it's only fair that you should all share. Listen!'

They listened eagerly while Peter told them what he had seen when he had climbed up to the balcony to get Susie's aeroplane.

'As soon as we saw the plane sitting so nicely on the balcony, I shinned up a tree to get it,' said Peter. 'And when I was there I noticed that there was a red glow shining in the balcony room. There was a crack in the curtains, you see, that's how I spotted the glow.'

'But what *was* the glow? Could you see?' asked Janet, eagerly.

'Yes. It came from a gas-fire, a *lighted* gas-fire!' said Peter. 'Now, what do you make of that?'

'Somebody left it on when the house was closed, and the people went abroad,' said Barbara, promptly. 'Easy!'

'Yes. That's what *I* thought at first,' said Peter. 'But now I'm not so sure. I have a sort of feeling that I was just about to notice something else odd when Jack suddenly called me, and I was scared the gardener would come back, so I rushed away to climb down the tree.'

There was a short silence. 'But what do you mean, you were *about* to notice something,' said Colin. 'What sort of something?'

'I don't know. I've been thinking and thinking, but it's like something in a dream. You nearly remember it and it slips away,' said poor Peter, frowning hard and trying to remember what it was that had so nearly ttracted his attention. 'I *think* it was something on a table.'

'A cloth,' said Barbara, not very brightly.

'Four legs,' said Pam, with a giggle.

. 'Don't be silly,' said Peter, impatiently. 'It was something *unusual*, I'm sure.'

'Well, what are we going to do about this gas-fire?' said George. 'It ought to be turned off, that's certain. It's a frightful waste of gas, and there might be a danger of fire from it.'

'That's what *I* think,' said Peter. 'But how do we get it turned off?'

'Tell the gardener!' said Jack, promptly. 'Or whoever's got the keys. I suppose, Peter, there can't be anyone in the house, can there? I mean, it *is* all locked up, isn't it?'

'Yes, as far as I know,' said Peter. 'All the curtains to the windows were drawn, anyhow, and that usually means a house is locked up. I wonder who the owners are?'

'Somebody called Hall,' said Jack. 'I heard my mother say so.'

'Would your mother know who had the keys?' asked Peter. 'I mean, sometimes people give the keys to neighbours, don't they? Or to estate agents?'

'She *might* know,' said Jack. 'I'll ask her. Suppose she says the estate agents have them, we could go and tell *them* about the gas-fire then. And if it's neighbours, perhaps my mother could telephone to them and get them to go in and turn off the fire.'

'And if we *can't* find out who has the keys, we'll have to tell that old gardener,' said Janet. 'For all we know, *he* has the keys himself! Perhaps he pops into the house and lights a gas-fire to warm his toes by when he's cold!'

'Fool!' said Peter. 'Look out, that's Scamper barking. Someone's coming!'

There was a knock on the door. 'If that's you, Susie, I'll pull your hair till you yell!' shouted Jack, fiercely.

But it wasn't Susie. It was Peter's mother. 'I don't know your password!' she called, 'but I've come to say that if you'd like to ask the Secret Seven to tea, Peter, they can all stay!'

'Mother! Come in! You don't need a password if you bring news like that!' said Peter, joyfully, and flung the door wide open. 'The meeting's over. Report any news from your mother tomorrow, Jack.'

[6]

A good half-hour's work

Next morning the Secret Seven met again, very promptly. The password was muttered five times to Peter and Janet in the shed, and five times Scamper barked a welcome.

'Well,' said Peter, when the door was shut and they were all sitting in a circle in the dark little shed. 'Any news to report, Jack?'

'Not much,' said Jack. 'I asked my mother about Bartlett Lodge, and she said the owners have gone abroad for a year, and they left the keys at their bank. Mother said no one is allowed to go into the house except by permission of the bank.'

'Really?' said Peter. 'Not to clean or anything?'

'I asked her that,' said Jack. 'And she said no, not even to clean. She said that Alice, a woman who comes to do some cleaning each week, went in and cleaned it thoroughly, top to bottom, before it was locked up.'

'Ah, then what about asking Alice if she left the fire on!' said Peter, at once. 'Couldn't you ask her that, Jack? Could you talk about the house and then sort of lead round to gas-fires and electric lights and so on?'

'Well, I don't mind trying,' said Jack. 'But wait a bit, no, I can't. She's broken her arm and isn't coming for a bit.'

'Bother,' said Peter. 'Now how can we get round *that*?'

Everyone thought hard. 'Why can't you go and ask her how she is, and take her some sweets or something?' said Janet at last. 'When our old nanny is ill we always pop round with a little present.'

'All right,' said Jack, feeling that he was being asked to do rather a lot. 'Anyway, why don't you all come with me? It would be easier then. She's seen most of you.'

'Perhaps on the whole it might make things easier if we *did* all go,' said Peter, considering. 'We could tell her about the aeroplane going into the garden. That would introduce the subject, so to speak. But we wouldn't say anything about climbing up to the balcony, of course.'

'Gosh no!' said Jack, horrified. 'She might tell my mother, and I'm sure I'd get into a row if she thought we'd gone there and climbed up like that!'

'Well, what about going straightaway?' said Peter, who liked doing things at once. 'Anyone got any money to buy sweets or something? We could buy her peppermints.'

'Oh, yes, Alice likes peppermints,' said Jack. 'That's a good idea. Come on – let's go. It's a lovely sunny afternoon, and I've had enough of this shed.'

So they all went out to buy the peppermints and were given quite a lot for a pound. Off they went to the little cottage down Green Lane where Alice lived. She was very pleased indeed to see them.

'Well, there now! It's a treat to see your smiling faces!' she said. 'And you're just in time to have one of my bits of gingerbread. As sticky as can be, it is, and I know Jack likes *that*!'

The children felt that Alice was giving them as much a treat as they hoped to give her with the peppermints! She was, however, so delighted with their unexpected gift that they couldn't help feeling pleased.

'And what have you been doing, you and Susie, since I broke my arm?' she said to Jack. 'Into mischief again, I'll be bound! And have you worn your cowboy-suit yet?'

This was a wonderful opening for what they wanted to say. Jack plunged in at once. 'Oh yes, and we've flown that lovely aeroplane that Susie got. And will you believe it, it flew right over the wall into Bartlett Lodge!'

'Did it, now? That's the house belonging to the Halls,' said Alice, offering the tin of gingerbread round generously. 'I cleaned it down from top to bottom after they went. My, that was a job!'

'Did you have to draw all the curtains?' asked Peter. 'We noticed they were drawn.'

'Yes, I drew them all,' said Alice. 'The house looked so dark and dreary then that I was glad to lock it up and leave it behind me!'

'I suppose you had to turn off the electricity and water and gas?' said Janet, feeling rather clever.

'Oh, yes, I turned everything off,' said Alice. 'So if any of you are thinking of moving in there, you'll have to get me to come and turn things on again for you!'

Everyone laughed heartily at this little joke, and Peter looked triumphantly at Jack as he, too, laughed. So the gas *had* been turned off, had it? Then how did that gas-fire come to be burning there, up in the balcony room? Well, they had learnt quite a bit from Alice!

'Isn't there *anyone* there?' asked Jack.

'Nobody at all. It's all locked up now. I tell you, I locked every window and door myself,' said Alice. 'The only person who goes there is old Georgie Grim, the garden-er, and a good name he's got too! Grim by name and grim by nature. But he's honest, I'll say that for him. Have another piece of gingerbread, Jack?'

'No thanks,' said Jack. 'We must be get-ting off. I hope your arm will soon be all right, Alice. Goodbye – see you soon again, I hope!'

And with that the Secret Seven marched off, feeling that they had done quite a good half-hour's work! And now, WHAT ABOUT THAT GAS-FIRE?

[7]

An unlucky encounter

'Let's go into this field and talk,' said Peter, as soon as they left Alice's house. 'We've learnt quite a few things from her. It was a good idea to go and see her. She's awfully nice, isn't she, Jack?'

'Yes. I told you she was,' said Jack. 'But look – if she locked and—'

'Wait till we're in the field,' said Peter. 'We don't want *anyone* to overhear this. At the moment it's our own little mystery, and we'll keep it to ourselves.'

So nobody said a word till they were all sitting down in the field. Then Peter began the talk.

'It's quite clear that *Alice* didn't leave the fire on,' he said. 'And if she did as she said, and turned off water, gas, and electricity when she left, then SOMEONE has turned on at least the *gas* since she locked up the house.'

'That's right,' said George. 'But who? And what for? Surely nobody is living in the house, unknown to anyone?'

'You'd have thought old Georgie Grim would have spotted any stranger about,' said Colin, thoughtfully. 'Alice said he was honest, didn't she? Well, if he'd noticed anyone lurking about, he'd surely have reported it?'

'I think he's horrid,' said Pam. 'I bet he wouldn't bother about reporting anything!'

'Don't be silly, Pam,' said Peter. 'Just because *we* think he's horrid, because he wouldn't let us get Susie's plane, isn't any reason to think he's dishonest.'

There was a silence. Nobody could think what should be done next.

'Do you think we should tell Mother?'

said Janet at last, turning to Peter. Peter hesitated.

'I don't think she'd believe I really *did* see that gas-fire burning,' he said. 'It sounds rather unbelievable after all that Alice told us.'

'Well, we can easily prove it's true,' said Jack. 'Easily! Let's wait till that gardener goes home for the night and slip over the wall and up that tree again. We can easily peep through the curtains.'

'Yes! And if the fire *is* burning there, though we know from Alice that the gas is turned off, *then* we'll tell your mother, Peter,' said George. Everyone nodded gravely.

'Yes. It's about the only thing to do,' said Peter. 'All right. Jack and I will scout round there this evening after Georgie Grim has gone home. Jack, I'll be round at your house about half-past six. It'll still be light, and we can shin up that tree in a second.'

'Who's going to boost us up the high wall?' said Jack. 'We can't climb it without help.'

Peter considered. 'Have you a light ladder you could lug out of your shed?' he asked. 'We could easily take it into the field – it's only just behind your house! And we could go up the ladder and clamber on the wall one after the other.'

'Right,' said Jack. 'I only hope Susie isn't about. If she sees me dragging a ladder out of the shed she'll stick to me like a leech to see where I'm going with it!'

'Bother Susie!' said Peter, feeling very glad that Janet was not like the tiresome Susie. 'Well, I'll see you about half-past six, Jack. We'll have a meeting tomorrow morning at ten-thirty, down in the shed.'

'Make it eleven,' said Colin. 'I've got to go to the dentist.'

'Right. Eleven o'clock,' said Peter. 'And tonight Jack and I will have a look at the

Mysterious Gas-Fire. I bet it will be burning away merrily!'

They all went home to their dinners, feeling pleasantly excited. Jack went to his garden-shed to see if there was a ladder there. Yes. There was the old one that his father used when he pruned some of the taller fruit trees.

'Hallo! What are you doing in here?' said Susie's voice, just behind him. He jumped, and Susie laughed.

'Oho! You've gone quite red! What are you up to?' said Susie, annoyingly. 'Are you doing some job for that silly Secret Seven club of yours? Do you want a ladder by any chance?'

Susie was altogether too good at guessing! Jack picked up a little fork and a basket and marched out. He would do some weeding and show Susie she was wrong about the ladder! She followed with great interest, calling out as she went.

'Oh, what a good little boy! He's going to do some weeding! And he doesn't know the difference between seedlings and weedlings!'

'Will you be quiet, Susie,' roared Jack, really exasperated, and pulled up a wallflower quite by mistake.

'That's a wallflower,' said Susie at once. 'Oooh, you *will* get into trouble if you're going to pull up all the wallflowers.'

And then Jack lost his temper and pulled up two more hefty wallflower plants and shook the earth from their roots all over his aggravating sister. Susie fled, howling in dismay.

At half-past six Peter came round to the garden door at Jack's home. He saw Jack waiting for him behind some bushes. He put his finger to his mouth to warn Peter to be quiet.

'Susie's about,' he whispered, and led the way to the shed on tiptoe. He opened the door and there, sitting half-way up the ladder he so badly wanted, was Susie, pretending to read a book, grinning all over her face!

'Hallo! You don't want the ladder, do you?' she said. 'I'll get down if you do.'

Jack glared at her, and then the two boys walked out and banged the door hard. 'Now we can't even have the ladder!' said Jack, fiercely. 'I'm so sorry, Peter.'

'Don't worry,' said Peter, cheerfully. 'We'll simply not go over the wall, that's all. We'll go in at one of the front gates. It can't be helped. Come on, and do cheer up, Jack. This may be rather exciting!'

The two boys made their way out of Jack's garden and walked across the field till they came to the little lane that led to the front of Bartlett Lodge. Now they were in the road into which the drive-gates opened. They looked cautiously up and down the road.

'Not a soul in sight,' said Jack. 'I think if we walked smartly up to the first drive-gate and darted inside we'd be safe from anyone's view. Come on. If anyone appears in the road we'll simply walk past the gates, and then come back again when the coast is clear.'

They walked quickly up to the first drive-gate. Nobody appeared at all, so they darted in quickly and hid in some bushes to make sure that no one had seen them. Nobody shouted at them, so they felt sure they were safe. Keeping carefully to the bushes, they made their way round the side of the big, silent house.

'It's a gloomy place, isn't it?' said Jack, in a low voice. 'The curtains are still drawn across every window. Now, look out! We've got to sprint across this yard, so be quick.'

They sprinted across the little yard, and ran straight into two big men! One was

Georgie Grim, and the other was a big, well-dressed man, wearing a suit, and carrying a slimly rolled umbrella. They both gaped at the two surprised boys.

'Here you! What are you doing here?' said the gardener at once, and pounced on Jack before he could get away. He gripped Jack's arm so hard that the boy cried out.

'Ha! You're the boy who said his aeroplane had flown into the garden, aren't you?' said Grim, and shook Jack as if he was a rat. 'Yes, you sat up on that wall and cheeked me! Now what are you doing here? If you—'

'Let me go!' cried Jack. 'You're hurting me.'

Grim shook him again. 'Yes, and I mean to! Was it you who came into this garden and walked over the bed at the bottom of that old tree? Was it you who climbed up the tree to the balcony? Oh, I saw the footmarks below, and I saw the marks where you'd climbed the tree! That I did! What were you doing up there, I'd like to know?'

'Our aeroplane landed on that balcony, that's all!' said Peter. 'We climbed the tree to get it. We couldn't help treading on the bed below, but there weren't any plants in it, only weeds!'

'Now look here, my lad,' said the other man in a pleasant, well-spoken voice, 'it's a serious thing to come trespassing into a private place, you know. And if this is the second time, as Grim here says, I'm afraid you're going to get into trouble. What are your names and addresses?'

Peter's heart sank. Gosh, now his father would hear about this and be angry, and Jack would get into trouble too.

'Honestly, sir, we weren't going to do any harm,' he said.

'Either you tell me honestly what you are doing here this evening, or I shall get Grim to go for the police – with you, boy, still in his grip,' said the stranger, sternly. 'I'm not the kind of person that lets bad boys get away with anything. If you tell me the truth, though, I may think twice about the police.'

'Well,' said Peter, desperately, 'I *will* tell you! Our aeroplane flew over the wall, and landed up there on that balcony. And Jack and I came to get it. I climbed up the tree to the balcony, and just as I was going to get down again, I had a look round at the balcony room, and I saw something odd.'

Both Grim and the stranger looked at him sharply. 'And what was the odd thing you saw?' asked the second man.

'The curtains up there don't quite meet,' said Peter. 'And when I peeped between them I saw a gas-fire burning in the room. I really did!'

'And we came back tonight to climb up again and see if it was still burning,' said Jack, still in Grim's steely grip. 'And if it was we were going to tell our parents, and they would ring up the police and—'

Grim gave a sharp exclamation. 'What! You saw a gas-fire burning? Impossible!' He turned to the other man. 'You're from the bank, aren't you? You've come to see if everything is all right? Well, it *is*, and what's more all the gas is turned off at the main, so this boy is telling lies! You can't have a gas-fire burning without gas!'

'I tell you I DID see it,' said Peter. 'And I was jolly astonished.'

'Well, this is a most amazing story,' said the man in the suit. 'I'm Mr Frampton, from the bank, and I came here to pay Grim his wages this evening and to see if everything was all right. You seem decent lads, not the little hooligans I thought you were at first. But really, if there's no gas it's difficult to believe your tale.'

'Have you got the keys with you?' asked Peter, eagerly. 'Couldn't you unlock the place, see if the gas really *is* turned off, and go up to that balcony room where I saw the fire? Just in case.'

'Hm, well, it seems rather a waste of time,' said Mr Frampton, putting his hands into his coat-pocket, and bringing out a Yale key labelled Bartlett Lodge No 2. 'But I think on the whole that I'd better go into this. Let that boy go, Grim. I'm inclined to believe they are not after any mischief. Now, where is the front-door key? Ah, here it is. We'll go in and see if there's any truth in this extraordinary tale!'

In a short while they were all in the big hall of Bartlett Lodge. Grim, looking as dour as his name, marched Mr Frampton to the kitchen, and showed him the gas-meter, the electricity switch, and the tap to the water main.

'Every one turned off, as you can see,' he said. Mr Frampton looked at them, and nodded.

'Right. Now let's go upstairs to this balcony room where the mysterious gas-fire is supposed to be burning. Lead the way, Grim, lead the way!'

[8]

Peter is very angry

Grim led the way, first up one wide flight of steps and on to a fine long corridor, and then up another flight of stairs to the second floor. The house seemed very dark because of the drawn curtains, and Mr Frampton stumbled once or twice. It smelt musty and shut up, too.

'Here's the balcony room,' said Grim, opening a door. A crack of light came in through the place where the curtains did not quite meet. Grim went across and drew them apart with a noise that made everyone jump.

Peter looked for the gas-fire. Yes, there it was, but no red light glowed from it! It stood there, unlit and cold! He stared at it in silence, unable to believe his eyes, for he had felt certain that it would be just as red and glowing as it had been when he had peeped in from the balcony and seen it.

Mr Frampton made a clicking noise of exasperation. 'Well! You've been making up a nice little story, haven't you, my boy? This fire is certainly not alight and can't have been before either, because all the gas is turned off. You should know better than to make up tales like that. I'm ashamed of you. You seem quite a decent lad, too. Well, Grim, shall we hand them over to the police and let them tell their fairy-tale to *them*, and see what the police have to say about it?'

Grim shook his head. 'I reckon the police have enough to do these days, without having to listen to silly tales like this. The boy made the whole thing up to amuse all his friends, and then made the tale an excuse to come trespassing.'

'I did *not*!' said Peter, angrily. 'And I'd like to tell you—'

'That's enough!' said Mr Frampton, sharply. 'And now, just listen to me. I will NOT have you children trespassing like this, whether it's to fetch balls or aeroplanes or anything. And I'm not listening to any more excuses or tales. If Grim had wanted to hand you over to the police I would have done so with pleasure, but he's let you off, and so will I – just this once! Grim, if you have any more trouble with these boys, ring me up and I'll deal with them.'

'Right,' said Grim, sounding extremely pleased.

'But I've got something else to—' began Peter, desperately, but Mr Frampton snapped at him at once.

'Silence! I will not listen to another word. I thought you were a decent lad. I'm mistaken, it seems. Get down the stairs and out of the gates before I chase you out with my umbrella.'

Peter gave Mr Frampton such a glare that Jack was quite astonished. Whatever was the matter with Peter? He had been proved wrong, so why did he go on arguing and interrupting? He took Peter's arm and pushed him to the stairway.

'Come on, idiot,' he said. 'Let's go while the going's good. You made a mistake. It's no use arguing about it!'

Looking very angry indeed, Peter went down the stairs with Jack, and out of the front door. He slammed it hard, and the noise echoed all around. It made Jack jump in fright, and he stared at Peter, really astonished.

'What *is* the matter?' he said. 'Surely you're not in a rage because you were proved wrong, Peter, old chap?'

Peter didn't answer. He took Jack's arm and led him at top speed down the drive and

into the road. He didn't say a word all the
way down the little lane to the field, and not
until they were well out in the middle of the
field did he open his mouth to the puzzled
and rather scared Jack.

Then he turned and faced him. 'So *you*
think I was mistaken too, do you?' he said.
'Well, I'm *not*. That fire was alight when I
saw it. I don't care tuppence if the gas and
the electricity and the water and everything
else is turned off – *that fire was alight*.
SOMEBODY had turned it on and lit it.
SOMEBODY had been in that room – and
done other things, besides lighting the gas,
too!'

Jack stared at Peter, amazed. '*What* other
things?' he said. 'And why didn't you tell
Mr Frampton?'

'I *tried* to. You know I did!' cried Peter.
'And everytime I tried he snapped at me and
shut me up! I shan't tell him anything! I'll
solve the mystery myself!'

'Wait a minute, Peter. Tell me. What other things did the person do besides lighting the gas-fire?' asked Jack, wondering if Peter had gone slightly mad.

'Listen. Do you remember I said that I had *almost* noticed something in that room, besides the gas-fire, yesterday morning?' demanded Peter. 'And I couldn't call to mind what it was because just as I was noticing it, you shouted at me?'

'Yes. I remember,' said Jack. 'What was it, then?'

'Well, I noticed a plant in a pot,' said Peter. 'A plant my mother grows in her greenhouse, called a primula. The flowers are rather like big polyanthus. And I noticed that the plant was alive and healthy, not all dead and withered as it *should* have been, left in an empty house for weeks. Primulas need a lot of water.'

'You mean someone had been watering it?' asked Jack.

'Yes,' said Peter, beginning to calm down. 'I looked into the pot just now and the soil was wet. Someone had watered it not later than yesterday. AND I noticed something else, which *you* should have noticed too if you'd been a *good* member of the Secret Seven!'

'What?' asked Jack, surprised again.

'I noticed that the clock on the mantelpiece was going,' said Peter. 'And it's only an eight-day clock. So *someone* must have wound it up during the last week, mustn't they? And I thought the room smelt of tobacco smoke too. Oh, somebody has been living in that room, I'm pretty sure!'

'Gosh!' said Jack, astounded. 'But who, Peter? And why?'

'That's for the Secret Seven to find out,' said Peter. 'Go round to everyone and remind them that there's an important, MOST IMPORTANT meeting at eleven o'clock sharp tomorrow morning. And don't let that tire-some Susie know a *thing* about it! This is very, very secret!'

[9]

Peter gives his orders

Again the Secret Seven were extremely punctual, and the password, 'Lollipops', was said briskly as all the members arrived at the meeting-shed, greeted excitedly by Scamper.

'What's up, Peter?' said George, seeing Peter's rather grim expression as he sat waiting in the shed for everyone. 'You look sort of boiling up inside.'

'Well, I am,' said Peter, relaxing into a short grin, and then looking grim again. Clearly something big was happening, and the Secret Seven settled down expectantly, feeling little thrills as they looked at their chief. Whatever was he going to tell them?

Very shortly and clearly Peter told them of his and Jack's visit to Bartlett Lodge, and how they had been caught by Grim the gardener and Mr Frampton from the bank, the man who held the keys of the locked house.

Then he told them how he had persuaded Mr Frampton to go into the house and find out whether the gas really was turned off or not (and what a sigh all the members gave when he had to confess that it *was* turned off after all); and then went on to describe how they had gone up to the balcony room, and seen the fire unlit (another disappointed sigh!) and then, and then . . .

The next part was truly exciting, of course, especially when he told about the ticking clock. The members gazed at Peter in real admiration. Here was a chief indeed! Why, he had behaved like a first-class detective, and he had stood up to Grim and the man from the bank like a hero!

'You should have *seen* Peter when he came out of that house!' Jack said, when Peter had finished his tale. 'He was in such a rage that he slammed the front door till it nearly fell off its hinges! And his face was as red as fire, and . . .'

'That's enough,' said Peter, his face looking almost as red as fire once again, he was so embarrassed at Jack's praises. 'Anyone would have felt as I did. Honestly, I kept *on* trying to tell Mr Frampton about the clock, and the plant, and the smell of smoke, but he simply wouldn't listen.'

'What a stupid man!' said Barbara. 'To think he could have noticed all those things and didn't. Still, *Jack* didn't notice any of them either, did he?'

'That's enough, Barbara,' said Peter again, seeing *Jack's* face go red now! 'We've got a most peculiar mystery on our hands, and we've got to get to the bottom of it ourselves. This is something that the Secret

Seven really *can* rack their brains over. Now, how can we find out who's been in the house, and if he was still there, hidden somewhere while Grim and Mr Frampton went in and out, and if Grim knows anything about it? And if anyone *is* hiding there, what's his reason?'

'We'd better try and find out if Grim really *has* got a name for honesty,' said George. 'If he has, and everyone speaks well of him, we'll know it's nothing to do with *him*.'

'Yes. That's a good point,' said Peter. 'Does anyone know somebody who has employed Grim at any time?'

'Yes. My granny did for a year,' said Pam. 'I didn't like him at all then, because he wouldn't let me pick even an unripe gooseberry when I went to tea with Granny!'

'Hm! That sounds rather honest than otherwise!' said Colin.

'Or mean!' said George. 'Hadn't Pam better go and ask her granny a few questions, Peter?'

'Yes. That's a job for you to do today, Pam,' said Peter, looking at her. 'I want a report this afternoon about that.'

'Right,' said Pam, feeling important, and writing it down in her notebook, though she knew she couldn't possibly forget.

'We really ought to find out where Grim lives and see if we can discover if he's at home each night,' said Peter. 'It might *possibly* be Grim making himself nice and comfortable at Bartlett Lodge. I mean, he might have a horrid wife who nags him, say, and he goes and sleeps in that house just to get away from her, now he's got the chance. I bet he knows how to get into the house, even though he hasn't got the keys.'

'I think that's a bit far-fetched,' objected Barbara. 'About his nagging wife, I mean.'

'We can't leave anything to chance,' said Peter, firmly. 'Nothing is too far-fetched to examine. Grim is an important person in this mystery. The more we know about him, the better.'

'All right,' said Barbara, hastily. 'But all I hope is that I don't have to go and interview a nagging wife!'

'Well, you *will*,' said Peter, to Barbara's horror. 'You and Janet can go together, once we've found out where he lives. Pam's granny will be able to tell her that, I expect.'

'Do we have to find out if Mr *Frampton* is all right?' asked Jack, beginning to feel that there was going to be a lot of snooping round in this mystery!

'Yes. I can ask my father that,' said Peter. 'I expect he'll know him, or know *of* him. But I don't somehow think Mr Frampton *really* comes into this.'

'What else do we do?' asked George.

'Well, when we've found out all we can about Grim, and have made up our minds about him, I shall probably decide to set a watch on Bartlett Lodge,' said Peter, in a most business-like tone. 'There's a good shed there, within view of the kitchen-door, which, I imagine, would be the likeliest place for any mysterious person to enter or leave the house. One or other of us must be on watch all the time. I am quite DETERMINED to track down the person who lives secretly in that balcony room.'

'It's terribly exciting,' said Pam, feeling quite breathless with all this sudden planning. 'I think you're a very good chief, Peter. I do really.'

'So do I,' said Jack, and the others agreed.

'Well, we'll soon see if I am or not,' said Peter, getting up. 'Time will tell! Oh, by the way, there's a new password for next time, as we've had our last one for a long time.'

'What is it?' asked Jack.

'Grim!' said Peter, smiling. 'Just that. Grim! And don't you forget it, anyone!'

[10]

The girls do very well

Pam felt very important as she went off to see her granny immediately after her mid-day dinner. She had her notebook in her pocket, and a freshly sharpened pencil. I may have to write down all kinds of details for Peter, she thought. What fun it is to belong to the Secret Seven. We just NEVER know what kind of job we'll have to do next.

Her granny was in her back garden, snipping off dead daffodils. She was very pleased to see Pam.

'Why, Pamela!' she said. 'I didn't expect you this afternoon. Have you come to have tea with me, dear?'

'No, I'm afraid not, Granny,' said Pam.

'I've got orders from Peter to interview you about someone.'

'Good gracious!' said Granny, surprised. '*Interview me*? What about?'

'About a gardener you once had, called Georgie Grim,' said Pam, taking out her notebook. 'You see, Granny, the Secret Seven is on to a mystery again, and we're interested in Grim because we think he's got something to do with the mystery.'

'You and your mysteries!' said Granny, laughing. 'You really amuse me. Well, well, if it's Peter's orders, you must do as you're told. Now, what do you want to know?'

'Was Grim honest, Granny, when he was with you?' asked Pam.

'Absolutely,' said Granny, and Pam wrote that down, wondering if she was spelling it right. 'Abslootly honest,' she wrote.

'Er – did he ever have to look after the house when you went away?' asked Pam.

'Yes. During the year that he worked for me, he and his wife came and lived in the house for a month, while we were away,' said Granny. 'And the wife kept the place spotlessly clean. She was a thin, pale woman, with a cough, I remember.'

'Wait a bit, you're going too quickly,' said Pam, writing down all this at top speed. 'How do you spell "spotlessly"? Oh, it's all right – I know.'

'Any more questions?' said Granny, amused. 'I feel as if you were a policeman questioning me, Pamela!'

Pam laughed. She was quite enjoying this, and couldn't help feeling that she was doing it very well. She bit the end of her pencil and wondered what to ask next.

'Er – did you miss anything from the house when you came back?' she said.

'Not a thing!' said Granny. 'And what was more, Mrs Grim had made a lot of jam for us, and bottled a great deal of fruit, and wouldn't take a penny for it, because she said she had enjoyed staying in the house so much. I must say the little woman looked a good deal better for the month she spent here. Dear me, am I going too fast for you, darling? Let *me* write it all down for you.'

'Oh, *no*,' said Pam at once. 'This is *my* job, Granny. Just say it all again slowly, and I'll soon get it down. Are there two Ts in "bottle", do you suppose?'

'There are usually,' said Granny. 'Well, well, I must say that I admire you Secret Seven. You certainly go into things thoroughly. *Do* stay to tea.'

'I wish I could, but Peter wants this information this afternoon,' said Pam. 'Well, thanks awfully, Granny. You've given me some surprising news. We all suspected Grim might be doing something he'd no right to do.'

'And what was that?' said Granny, quite overcome with curiosity.

'Oh, it's a secret,' said Pam. 'We're never supposed to talk about our mysteries while we're solving them. Goodbye, Granny, and thank you very much.'

She skipped off happily, her notebook safely in her pocket. Pam was not often entrusted with important things by Peter, and she felt rather proud of the way she had written down Granny's answers to her questions. In fact, she thought herself quite clever!

Peter and the three boys were in the shed with Scamper when Pam arrived. 'Lollipops!' she said, as she knocked at the door. There was no answer.

'Let me in!' called Pam. 'I said the password.'

'You didn't, whoever you are,' called Peter's voice.

'I'm Pam, and you *know* it's me!' said Pam indignantly. 'I've got a lot of news. Let me.'

'Password, please,' said Peter.

'But I've already s—' began Pam, and then she suddenly remembered the *new* password. 'Oh, sorry, Peter – Grim, Grim, GRIM!'

'Once is quite enough,' said Peter, and opened the door. 'Well, did you see your granny?'

'Yes,' said Pam, and beamed round happily. 'Here are my notes, with my questions and Granny's answers. I wrote everything down.'

Peter took the notes and read them out aloud, much to Pam's delight. He shut the little notebook and nodded at Pam.

'Very good, Pam. A very nice piece of work. Well, it seems as if Grim is honest enough, and his wife too. In fact the wife sounds really nice. It's rather surprising, really, because I couldn't help feeling that bad-tempered old Grim was the one who had broken into Bartlett Lodge somehow.

Now it seems as if somebody *else* must be there, someone that Grim knows nothing about, for if he did he would certainly report it, as your granny says he's absolutely honest.'

'It's funny, isn't it?' said George. 'Well, we'll certainly have to find out who it is.'

'Yes, we must keep a watch on the kitchen-door, as I said,' decided Peter. 'Hallo, here comes Janet and Barbara. They've been to find out about Mrs Grim. I wonder if they'll remember the new password!'

A knock came at the door. 'Grim,' said Janet's voice, and then came a giggle. '*Mr Grim.*'

'And *Mrs* Grim!' said Barbara. Peter opened the door, grinning.

'Come in, idiots,' he said, 'and tell us your news!'

The two girls came in and sat down. Scamper gave them an enormous welcome.

'Hallo, Pam!' said Janet. 'What did your granny say about Grim?'

'Oh, she says he's absolutely honest,' said Pam. 'Here are my notes about it. I wrote them down.'

Janet and Barbara were impressed with the notes. 'You didn't spell the word "absolutely" the right way,' pointed out Barbara. 'Oh, Peter, *we* didn't make notes. We only just asked questions and remembered the answers.'

'That's all right,' said Peter. 'Janet, what happened? Make your report, please.'

'Well, we went down to where Grim lives,' said Janet. 'I found out from the postman; it was quite easy. Oh, Peter, it's a *dreadful* little cottage. Really dreadful.'

'Why? What's it like?' asked Peter.

'It's near the canal, and built so low that it's on a level with the water,' said Janet. 'And you know we've had a lot of rain this year, so the canal water has risen quite a bit, and it has overflowed into the little cottage garden . . .'

'And the ground floor of the cottage must be TERRIBLY damp,' said Barbara. 'And do you know, we even saw fungus growing all the way up one wall! It's really horrible.'

'It's in very bad repair too,' said Janet. 'Daddy would never let *his* cottages get like that, Peter. Our farm-men's cottages are palaces compared with Grim's. I can't think how he stands it. There's quite a big hole in the roof, where some tiles have fallen off.'

'No wonder they were so happy when they looked after my granny's house one summer,' said Pam. 'And no wonder Granny said Mrs Grim looked thin and ill. Anyone would, if they lived in that damp, smelly cottage down by the canal!'

'I wonder they don't move,' said Jack.

'Well, it's hard to get a cottage these

days,' said George, 'especially at a low rent. Did you find out anything about Mrs Grim, Janet? Did you see her?'

'No, we didn't,' said Janet, 'but we talked to the woman next door. Her cottage is built much higher than the Grims', and it's quite dry. She saw us looking round the Grims' place, and called out to know what we wanted.'

'And we just said we were looking at the quaint old cottage!' said Barbara. 'Which was perfectly true, of course. And we asked her who lived there, though *we* knew it was Grim's cottage.'

'You did well,' said Peter, approvingly. 'Go on. What did the woman tell you?'

'Well, she told us what we already knew – that Grim has a daily job, keeping that big garden going at Bartlett Lodge, and that he comes home about six o'clock each night. And that his wife isn't well, so he does all the shopping in his dinner-hour, and cooks a meal at night. And she said that Mrs Grim was a nice little woman . . .'

'And she's very fond of Grim,' said Barbara, anxious not to be left out. 'Gosh! Fancy anyone being fond of surly old *Grim.*'

'Mrs Grim must be quite ill,' said Janet. 'Her neighbour says she hasn't been out to hang her washing up for a whole week. Grim even does that, too!'

'Well, *I* think he sounds rather a nice old boy, even though he's so bad-tempered with us,' said Peter, rather astonished at all this news. 'Pam's granny says he's quite *honest*, and if he does all that for his wife, he must be kind as well.'

'I expect it's living in that dreadful damp cottage that makes him surly,' said Barbara, who really had been shocked to think of anyone living in such a horrid little hole. 'Peter, you wouldn't even let one of your *pigs* live in a place like that.'

'I should think not!' said Peter. '*Our* pigs have wonderful sties, and they're cleaned out twice a day.'

It suddenly began to dawn on everyone that their reports had not helped the mystery in the least. In fact, what they had learnt actually wiped Grim right out of the picture, and left them with nobody to suspect at all, except perhaps Mr Frampton, the man from the bank. But Peter had something to say about him.

'*He's* all right. My father's known him for years,' said Peter. 'I just mentioned casually that I'd met him, and Dad said, "Oh, Frampton, he's a fine chap, quite a friend of mine. Where did you meet him?"'

'Gosh, what did you say to *that*?' asked Jack, remembering their meeting with the man, and how nearly they had got into serious trouble. 'How did you answer?'

'Well, Scamper barked at that very moment, and I just didn't answer the question, but asked Scamper one instead!' said Peter, with a laugh. 'I said, "Who's coming, Scamper, who's coming, old boy? Let's go and see who you're barking at!" And out of the room we went.'

There was another silence. A cold, flat feeling slowly came over the Seven. Where did they go from here? Was there anything they could do to solve the mystery now, except what Peter had suggested before – watch the kitchen-door of Bartlett Lodge from the little shed opposite it? But they *knew* it wasn't Grim going into the house. Would they ever see any intruder at all? They couldn't watch the doors and windows! It would have been easy enough just to watch the kitchen-door when they felt sure it was Grim going in and out; but suppose the intruder, whoever he was, never came and went at all, but simply stayed hidden in the house, turning on the gas at the main whenever he wanted a little warmth, or to boil a kettle!

'Let's talk and plan,' said Peter, at last. 'Now, has anyone a good idea, a really good one?'

No one said a word at first, and then Jack spoke up. 'Well, Peter, the only thing *I* can think of is for one of us to climb that tree up to the balcony tonight, and watch for a light to come on in that room, and peep through the crack in the curtains to see who it is. That's my idea!'

[11]

An astonishing discovery

The rest of the Seven stared at Jack in admiration. 'Why ever didn't we think of that before?' said Peter. 'Of course whoever is hiding there would feel quite safe at night, with Grim gone home, and nobody about at all. We might see something really interesting if we watch up on the balcony!'

'Bags I go,' said George, at once.

'*Four* of us will go,' said Peter. 'One of us must be on guard at the gate to warn the others if someone comes in there. We don't want to be caught. One of us must also be at the bottom of the tree to warn the ones on the balcony if anyone comes. I think Jack and I will climb the tree and be the balcony watchers – we've been up there before.'

'Can I come too?' said Janet, longingly. 'It's beginning to sound awfully adventurous!'

'No you can't come,' said Peter, 'or there will be too many. The four of us will go together when it's really dark.'

'Let's ask if we can go to the cinema,' said Jack. 'And not stay till the end, but slip out about eight o'clock and go to Bartlett Lodge.'

'Good idea,' said Peter. 'Right, we'll all meet at the cinema. You others can come too, if you're allowed, but you'll have to sit right through the programme, if your parents will let you stay as late as that.'

'Mine won't,' said Barbara, sadly. 'At least I don't think so. Oh, I shan't be able to sleep tonight for wondering what's happening to you four boys.'

A very pleasant feeling of excitement warmed the hearts of the Secret Seven for the rest of that day. Even Scamper felt it, and was most bitterly disappointed when Janet and Peter went off to the cinema without him after tea.

He sat down sadly in a corner. Now he would have a long, long wait till he could bark and jump and wag his tail again!

None of the Secret Seven paid that much attention to the picture at the cinema, and yet it was a good one, all about a wild pony, the kind they usually loved. The four fidgeted and looked at their watches, wishing the time would go quickly, so that they might leave, and go about their night adventure!

At ten to eight Peter whispered to Jack. 'We'll go! I can't sit still a moment longer! Tell the others.'

Peter led the way. It was dark outside now, and they needed their torches. It was a cloudy night and not even a star showed in the sky.

They made their way to Jack's house and

slipped in at the back gate. 'Watch out for Susie!' said Jack, in a low tone. 'She's in tonight.'

But there was no sign of the aggravating Susie, much to Peter's relief. They went across the field at the back of Jack's house and down the little lane into the road beyond, where Bartlett Lodge stood.

'Now,' said Peter, halting. 'You know your orders, all of you. Colin, watch by the gate. Hoot like an owl if anyone comes in. George, you're to stand at the foot of the tree that we're going to climb to the balcony. You're to hoot too, if you see or hear anything suspicious. Jack, have you got your torch ready? We'll need it to climb the tree.'

Jack put his torch between his teeth, and so did Peter, as soon as they began to climb the tree that grew up to the second-floor balcony. This meant that they could use both their hands for climbing, and yet could see where they were going, though rather awkwardly.

Colin was at his post by the gate, hiding behind a bush. George was at the foot of the tree, listening intently for any unusual sound. He could hear Jack and Peter cautiously climbing the tree. Then he could hear the slight scrape of their rubber shoes as they climbed over the stone balcony. Now a great disappointment for Peter and Jack – no longer could they see through the crack in the curtains! Someone had pulled them carefully together, so that not the tiniest chink remained for them to peep through! The boys were bitterly disappointed!

'Look at that! We can't possibly see into the room now,' whispered Jack.

'Yes, but it shows someone has been into the room again!' said Peter. 'It may even mean that somebody is there *now*.'

They pressed their noses against the closed window, trying in vain to see inside.

They saw nothing, but they suddenly heard sounds, sounds which surely came from the inside of that little room!

'Listen!' whispered Jack. 'What is it?'

'It's a radio being played very, very quietly,' said Peter. 'We can hardly hear it. I'm sure that's what it is. Would you believe it! Who in the world is in there?'

They had now switched off their torches, and were in complete darkness. They stood there, wondering what to do. How did the intruder get into the house? Mr Frampton appeared to be the only one with the keys of the house; not even Grim had one. And anyway they had proved that he was absolutely honest. Then had some outsider a key? Or did he perhaps get in through a coal-hole? Or was there an unfastened window somewhere? All these things went through the boys' minds very quickly, and then something happened that made them jump violently.

An owl's hoot sounded from the front of the house! It must be Colin giving the arranged warning. The two boys stiffened at once. And then, to their horror, another hoot came, this time so near to them that they jumped in fright again. It came from the bottom of the tree.

'Danger!' said Peter. 'Keep quite still, Jack. Something's going to happen!'

The two boys on the balcony stood absolutely still, and hardly breathed. And then they heard a sound that made them stiffen again in fright.

'Someone's climbing up the tree!' whispered Peter to Jack. 'I can hear him – and see the light of his torch!'

'What can we do?' said Jack, trembling. 'He will see us here. We can't hide anywhere on this balcony.'

'No. But we can quickly scramble up the tree a bit higher and hide in the leaves,' said Peter, pulling Jack to the tree. He could now hear the climber's heavy breathing farther down the tree. Thank goodness he was slow at climbing!

'Quiet now!' whispered Peter, as he and Jack climbed back into the tree and further upwards. They then stayed quite still, peering through the leaves down at the balcony below.

A man was climbing up the tree to the balcony, his torch in his mouth. As he came, a warning owl-hoot sounded again from below. The man was now climbing over the little stone pillars of the balcony, and stood below the boys, taking his torch from his mouth. Jack and Peter in the tree above could see the light shining brightly.

The man went to the window and knocked. It was a special knock – three long ones, two short ones and then two long ones. Knock-knock-knock. Knock-knock. Knock-knock.

The boys held their breath and peered

through the leaves cautiously. They saw the curtains drawn back from the window, and immediately a light streamed out from the room inside. Then someone unfastened the window and opened it.

As the light streamed out on to the balcony, Jack and Peter saw the man who stood there, saw him quite clearly and recognised him! They could hardly believe their eyes!

The man went swiftly through the window, shut it behind him and drew the curtains across so that not a chink of light showed. Only when the window was shut did the two boys dare to breathe. Then Peter clutched Jack.

'Did you see who it was, Jack?'

'Yes. *Surely* it was old Grim the gardener!' said Jack, quite astounded. 'What did *you* think?'

'Yes – it *was* Grim! But who would have thought it! *Grim*! The honest Grim! No wonder he was angry when he discovered our footmarks at the bottom of this tree, and saw that *we* had climbed it too, and had used his own private way into the house!'

'But who's *in* there?' said Jack, feeling bewildered. 'It must be the someone who lit the gas-fire and wound up the clock, and watered that plant! Is it some burglar there busy packing up things for Grim to take away?'

'Goodness knows!' said Peter, as puzzled as Jack. 'I suppose it was Grim who had carefully turned off the gas at the main last night when we all went in to see the house. He must have seen our footmarks under the tree by then and have been afraid we might have seen the gas-fire and tell tales about it. So he quietly turned off the gas at the main, in case anyone said they'd seen the fire, because it's plain there couldn't be a fire without gas. I was jolly puzzled about that, weren't you?' 'Very,' said Jack. 'Well, what do we do now? Better climb down, I think, because I'm sure we can't see anything more here at the moment. We'd better find Colin and George – they'll be worried about us.'

So they climbed carefully down the tree again, making no noise at all, nor daring even to switch on their torches. They felt carefully with their feet before they made a step downwards, and were soon at the bottom.

There was no sign of George. 'He may think we are the man who climbed up,' whispered Jack. 'What about saying our password, Peter? He'll know it's us, then.'

'I was just going to,' said Peter. 'Grim!' he said, in a piercing whisper. 'Grim!'

'Here I am!' said George, from a nearby bush. 'Gosh, I was glad to hear the password! I was afraid it might be that man again! Did you hear my hoot?'

'Yes. And Colin's too,' said Peter. 'Let's

go and find him. This mystery has got very mysterious, all of a sudden!'

They found Colin hidden by the front gate, and gave him the password. He appeared as soon as he heard it. They all slipped out of the gate and down the road, and were soon in the little lane leading to the field behind Jack's house.

They stopped in the middle of the field, having been completely silent since leaving the front gate.

'Who was that man? Did you see?' said Colin at once.

'It was Grim!' said Peter. 'Would you believe it! Grim, the man we had ruled out completely. What *can* he be doing there?'

'Pretty mean of him to leave his sick wife all alone each night in that horrible cottage,' said Colin. 'He must have a pal in Bartlett Lodge and be planning to rob the house in peace and quiet while the owners are away.

There's nothing to stop them taking things bit by bit.'

'Shall we tell the police?' asked George.

'I don't know. I rather think I'll tell my father,' said Peter. 'You see, he knows Mr Frampton, the man who has the keys of the place. We'd better leave it to them as to what to do. Gosh, who'd have thought it was Grim after all!'

'Well, I never liked him,' said Colin. 'Horrid, bad-tempered man. Come on, let's get on. I'm beginning to feel as if there may be quite a lot of Georgie Grims in this dark field, waiting to pounce on us. Hurry up!'

'We'll go to my house and tell my father straightaway,' said Peter. 'You must all come with me. There'll be a lot to tell, and you'll have to back me up. Let's go by the cinema and see if the others are out. They really ought to be in on this.'

They went down the road that led to the

cinema, and saw the people streaming out – and the three girls with them! Peter ran up.

'Hey, you three! You're to come with us. Something very strange has turned up, and we're all going to my house to tell my father. *He'll* know what to do!'

[12]

Peter's father takes over

The four boys told the excited girls what had happened. When they came to the part where Jack and Peter had actually heard someone climbing up to the very balcony on which they were standing, Pam gave a loud squeal.

'Oh! I should have been scared stiff! Oh, who was it? I'm jolly glad I wasn't there!'

'It was old Georgie Grim!' said Peter. 'What do you think of *that*? And to think we'd quite decided that he was honest and kind and all the rest of it! Anyway, it's a serious matter now. That's why we're going back to tell my father.'

Peter's father and mother were most astonished to see everybody coming in

together. 'Why Colin – Jack – Pam, Barbara, George – whatever are you doing
back here instead of going home?' said
Peter's mother.

'Mother, we've got something to tell
you,' said Peter. 'Dad, you'll be surprised
when you hear it! You see, the Secret Seven
have—'

'Don't tell me you've tumbled into another adventure!' said his father. 'You haven't got yourselves into trouble, have you?'

'Oh, no,' said Peter. 'And – well, I hope
you won't be cross when you hear the
things we've done.'

'Begin at the beginning,' said his mother,
taking down a tin of biscuits and handing
them round. 'You're the chief of the Seven,
aren't you, Peter? Well, you begin, then.'

So Peter began the strange story, right
from the morning when Susie's aeroplane
had flown over the wall into the garden of
Bartlett Lodge, and disappeared. He told of

the angry gardener, of how he and Jack had discovered the aeroplane on the balcony and climbed up to get it . . .

'And it was *then* that the mystery really began,' said Jack, interrupting. 'Wasn't it, Peter? Because when Peter peeped in between the drawn curtains of the balcony windows he saw a gas-fire merrily burning away there!'

How astonished Peter's parents were to hear the story and to listen to the way the Seven had proved Grim's honesty, and his kindness to his wife, and then, to cap everything, they heard the astonishing ending!

'There we were, up in the tree six foot above the balcony, trying to see who it was coming knocking on the window of that curtained room, and when the curtains were pulled and the light streamed out we saw who it was.'

'And who *was* it?' said Peter's father, really excited.

'It was *Grim*,' said Peter. 'Yes, it really was, Dad! Someone from inside opened the window, and he got in, and the curtains were drawn across and the window fastened!'

'And we thought we'd better come and tell you because you know Mr Frampton, who has the keys,' said Jack. 'We felt sure you would know the best thing to do.'

'That was sensible of you,' said Peter's father. 'Well, I'm blessed! The things you Seven get up to! And yet I can't find fault with you for anything you've done in this matter. You were very sensible and most courageous, and now, of course, we must at once go after this fellow Grim, and see what he's up to. Thanks to you, we shall catch him in his lair with his burglarious friend, whoever he is!'

'His burglarious friend!' said Pam. 'That sounds exciting. What are you going to do, please?'

'I'm going to ring up Mr Frampton, get him to come round with the keys of Bartlett Lodge, and he and I will go together to surprise Grim and his friend in their cosy lair,' said Peter's father, getting up to go to the telephone.

'Dad! Dad, can we go too?' cried Peter, afraid that at this most exciting moment he was going to be left out.

'I'll see what Mr Frampton says,' said his father, and dialled his number. The children listened to the one-sided conversation in silence, their hearts beating fast. What an adventure this had suddenly turned into! Oh, if only they were allowed to see the end of it!

Peter's father rang off and turned to the waiting children. 'Mr Frampton is extremely interested, as you can imagine. He's coming round straight away and will pick me up here in his car. He says Peter and Jack may come too, as they will be able to state again that they actually saw the gas-fire burning the day before yesterday. They'll be what we call witnesses.'

'Can't we others come?' said Janet, dolefully. 'Oh, I do want to, Dad.'

'I dare say you do,' said her father. 'But you must realise that we can't have the whole Seven of you trailing after us in what may be quite a serious matter. Mr Frampton is going to ring up the police, and ask them to stand by in case he telephones from Bartlett Lodge for help. We shall have to find out first if it really *is* a police matter – and it probably is.'

Jack and Peter felt a great big surge of excitement welling up inside them. They grinned at one another in joy. They were going to be in at the end. What would happen? What would Grim say? And who was his 'burglarious friend'?

In a few minutes there came the sound of a car hooting at the front gate. Peter, his father, and Jack hurried out, followed by the envious gazes of the others. Then Janet's mother set to work to ring up the other children's parents and tell them not to worry; the Secret Seven were at her house!

Jack and Peter got into Mr Frampton's car, and sat silently in the back. They still remembered how angry he had been with them only a short time ago! He said nothing to them, but spoke briefly to Peter's father, and then drove off to Bartlett Lodge.

Jack squeezed Peter's arm in excitement. 'We're bang in the middle of a real adventure!' he said, in a low voice. 'Whatever do you suppose is going to happen next?'

[13]

Inside the empty house

The car drew up outside Bartlett Lodge. The house looked absolutely dark, not a light to be seen anywhere. They all got out, and Mr Frampton spoke quietly as they stood beside the car.

'I propose that I unlock the front door, and that we all go in silently,' he said. 'It is imperative that we make no noise at all, for we don't want to give any warning to those fellows inside. We will go straight up to the same room that these boys took me up to before and surprise the men there, and demand an explanation. Now, follow me.'

They followed him in at the drive-gate, and up to the front door. He cautiously slid the key in, turned it, put a second key into a lock below, and turned that also. The door opened with a small creak.

Mr Frampton walked in quietly. The others followed, and he shut the door silently. He switched on his torch and spoke in a whisper.

'The telephone is here, in that corner. You, boy – what's your name, now?'

'Peter,' said Peter.

'Well, you, Peter, will have to be the one to nip down to the phone and call the police if we have any trouble,' said Mr Frampton. 'Just say that I want someone sent along here at once. Is that clear?'

'Yes,' said Peter, and again felt the uprush of breathless excitement that all adventures bring.

'Now, quiet,' said Mr Frampton, and led the way upstairs, his torch shining steadily in front of him. The stairs were well carpeted, and their footsteps made no noise at all. The men went first, the two boys followed. Jack was so excited that he felt quite breathless.

Up the first flight of stairs, on to the wide landing, and then very, very quietly up the second flight. Again there was a landing, but not such a wide one. Mr Frampton stood quite still at the top, and then switched off his torch.

A line of light showed under one door, the door of the balcony room! From inside came a murmur of voices and then suddenly the voices became raised, and the four outside could hear shouts and threats!

What was going on in that closed room? Jack felt himself shaking at the knees. 'It's all right,' whispered Mr Frampton, feeling Jack trembling against him. 'They've got the radio on, they're listening to a play. Don't be scared!'

Jack was most relieved. Only the radio! Of course! He and Peter had heard it before, when they had stood outside on the balcony! Mr Frampton now strode forward to the closed door and turned the handle, but he turned it in vain! The door was locked on the inside!

Mr Frampton raised his hand and knocked most imperiously on the door, shouting at the same time, 'Open this door at once!'

The radio in the room was switched off suddenly and now there was nothing but silence. Mr Frampton knocked again. 'I said OPEN THIS DOOR!'

'Who's there?' said a voice from inside.

'Open the door, and you'll soon see,' roared Mr Frampton, making both boys jump violently. 'I know your voice, Grim! The game's up. Open the door, or it will be the worse for you and your friend!'

There was a silence for a few seconds, and then Grim's voice came again, sounding most upset. 'It's you Mr Frampton, isn't it? You haven't got the police with you, have you? You know I'm an honest man, you—'

'I've no police here at the moment,' thundered Mr Frampton, 'but I'm sending someone down to telephone them in one minute's time, if you do not open this door! As for your honesty, I fear it will be difficult for you to prove that, Grim.'

There sounded a hurried few words from inside the room, as if Grim were reassuring someone. Then he spoke again, in a most beseeching voice.

'Mr Frampton, I'll open the door and come out to you, if you'll let me shut it after me and will not come into the room till I've spoken to you.'

'You'll open this door, and we shall come in straightaway,' said Mr Frampton, angrily. 'What nonsense is this? And I warn you, Grim, that if you let your friend get away through that window it will be the worse for you. Have done with this nonsense, man, and OPEN – THIS – DOOR!'

The door still did not open. Mr Frampton turned to Peter and spoke to him in a loud voice, so that Grim could hear it inside the room.

'Peter, go down into the hall and ring up the police as I told you. Tell them to send someone here immediately.'

'Right,' said Peter, but before he could take more than two steps there came a cry from Grim.

'No! Don't get the police! I'll open the door. Wait, wait!'

'Wait, Peter,' said Mr Frampton, in a low voice. 'I think he's come to heel.'

Nobody moved. They heard a key turning in the lock on the other side of the door, the handle turned, and the door opened. Grim stood there, his surly face lined and worried.

'Once more, I beg of you, don't come into

this room,' he said, holding the door so that no one could see into the room. 'I do beg of you.'

'Stand aside, man,' said Mr Frampton, and pushed him sternly to one side. He stepped into the room, followed by Peter's father. The two boys came last, wondering whatever they were going to see.

Nobody in the least expected to see what was there! They stood silent, staring in astonishment.

[14]

A great surprise

The little balcony room looked clean and cosy. The gas-fire burned steadily, and the clock on the mantelpiece ticked merrily. The table was set with a small white cloth, and on it was a loaf of bread on a wooden platter, a dish of butter, and a plate of yellow cheese.

But these were not the things that surprised the four visitors. Their eyes were fixed on one corner of the room, where there was a couch near the fire. On it lay a woman, a little old woman with white hair and white face, whose hands trembled as her scared eyes watched the four come into the room.

Mr Frampton stopped abruptly in astonishment. He, like the others, had expected to see another man, some 'burglarious friend'. But there was no one to see except the frightened old woman.

'Please,' she said, in a trembling voice. 'Please, it's all my fault. Don't be hard on Georgie.'

Mr Frampton spoke in a surprisingly kind voice. 'Now don't get upset, old lady. We've only come to see what's happening here.'

Tears suddenly rolled down the old woman's cheeks. Grim went over to her and took her hand. 'Now, now,' he said, 'don't you fret. I did it for the best.'

Then he turned to Mr Frampton. 'You see, it was like this. My wife, she's not strong, and her cough has been bad all winter. The doctor said I'd have to take her away from that cottage of ours, too damp he said it was, and he said he'd get her into a hospital . . .'

'And I wouldn't go,' said the old woman. 'I can't be separated from Georgie. I'd die, I know I would.'

'And then the canal water rose with all the rain we had, and the water came into the house,' said Grim, in a desperate voice. 'And some tiles came off and the rain came through into our bedroom. Well, what was a man to do? I couldn't find another place to go to, and here was this big house, all empty, and we only need one small room, and I was at work here . . .'

'I see,' said Mr Frampton, sitting down on a chair. 'Yes, I see. So you managed to get your wife here, into a warm, dry room, and you turned on the gas and the electric light and the water . . .'

'Yes. I got in through the coal-hole the first time, and went up into the kitchen, and unlocked the door,' said Grim. 'You had taken the key, but I knew where a spare one hung on a hook on the dresser. And I brought my old wife here one night, and a terrible walk it was for her . . .'

'And you made her comfortable here, Grim?' said Mr Frampton. 'And did the shopping, and the washing, and hung it out behind your old cottage? Yes, I know all about that, you see! And then you climbed in each night through the balcony window.'

'Yes,' said Grim, dolefully. 'And I was in a rare temper with these boys here, when I knew they'd been up that tree outside, and on to the balcony, and what a fright I had when they told you about seeing the little gas-fire here. I tell you, I've been in a real state all the time. Yes, I know I did wrong, but what was a man to do?'

'You could have come and asked me, Grim,' said Mr Frampton.

'And you'd have said no!' cried Grim. 'Look here, and you too,' he said, turning to Peter's father. 'My old woman, she's done what she could in the house while she's been here. She's dusted every day, ill as she is, and she's watered every plant, and she's polished every bit of furniture. She was scared to death all the time, but I will say this, her cough's better.'

Peter suddenly found that there were tears in his eyes. Poor Grim! And his poor, ill old wife, in that dreadful damp cottage with a hole in the roof. After all, they had done no harm. In fact, Mrs Grim had dusted and polished and watered, and done as much as she could!

There was a little silence. Then Mr Frampton spoke in a gentle voice. 'Well, Grim, I shall have to report this to the owners, of course, but I shall point out your difficulties, and say that Mrs Grim has kept the house dusted and polished, and . . .'

'You won't get the police, will you?' pleaded the little old woman, from her couch. 'My Georgie, he's a good man, honest as the day, and kindness itself. He's got a temper that gets him into trouble now and again, but he's a good honest man, and *I* ought to know!'

'I shan't get the police,' said Mr Frampton. 'But as you know, perhaps, the owners are coming back next week. You will not be able to stay here then.'

'I'll go back to my old cottage then,' said Mrs Grim. 'My cough's better since I've been here, this warm, dry place. I'll be all right now in our cottage.'

'You won't!' said Grim, suddenly sounding desperate again. 'They'll put you somewhere away from me. They'll say you're ill, and they'll take you away!'

'Now, listen, stay here until I hear from the owners,' said Mr Frampton. 'I can see you are to be trusted. But if you're in trouble another time, ask for help from some friend, Grim. Don't do things like this.'

'I'd have done that, but I thought my wife might be taken away from me,' said Grim. 'I'm sorry for the trouble I've caused, but we've done no harm, that I can promise you.'

Peter's father stood up. 'Come along, Frampton,' he said. 'Let's leave them in peace. Grim, come along to me tomorrow and I'll see that you are supplied with milk and eggs for your wife. Good night, Mrs Grim. Cheer up. We'll see what can be done for you and Grim. Good night, Grim.'

'Good night,' said Grim, and the two men, followed by the two boys, went out of the room, leaving Grim standing at the door, worried and anxious.

'Dad!' said Peter, looking as anxious as the old gardener. 'Dad, can't we do *something*? I shan't be happy till we do!'

[15]

Three cheers for
the Secret Seven!

The next morning there was another Secret Seven meeting in the old shed. One after another the knocks came, and the password.

'Grim!'

'Grim! It's me, Pam.'

'Grim! Can I come in?'

Peter opened the door five times, and Scamper barked five times too. Soon everyone was there. They all looked rather nervous, for the events of the night before had surprised and shocked them.

'To think that we hated Grim so much, and all the time he was worried in case we found out his poor, precious secret!' said Janet.

'I *can't* bear to think of them having to go back to that awful cottage,' said Barbara. 'Old Mrs Grim will get a dreadful cough again. But they'll have to turn out of Bartlett Lodge in a few days. Oh dear, this mystery is having a rather horrid end.'

'We've GOT to do something to help them,' said Jack. He pulled a purse out of his pocket, and emptied some money on to the top of a wooden box. 'Look, I've emptied my money-box and Susie's too, and I've brought all the money along in case it will be any use.'

'*Susie's* money-box!' said Janet, amazed. 'But did she say you could?'

'Yes. I told her all about last night when I got home,' said Jack. 'After all, you know, it *was* her aeroplane that started this adventure. Wasn't it?'

'Yes,' said everyone, nodding.

'So I thought Susie ought to hear the

story,' said Jack. 'And she told me to take *all* her money, too.'

'Gosh! People are most surprising!' said Barbara. 'Good old Susie!'

'Well, now,' said Peter, 'does everyone want to give money to help the Grims? And is there anything else we can do? I dare say our money would help to mend that hole in the cottage roof. We've got to do *some-*thing! I shan't feel happy till we've tried to make up for spying on old Grim, and bring-ing his precious secret to light.'

Everyone most willingly agreed to help. Peter felt proud of his Secret Seven. There wasn't a mean, ungenerous person among them! Jolly good!

Scamper suddenly began to bark, and a knock came at the door.

'Password!' shouted Peter.

'I don't know it,' said his father's voice.

'Oh, it's you, Dad! We'll let you in with-out the password!' said Peter, and opened the door. His father came in, and smiled round at everyone. He saw the money on the top of the box and raised his eyebrows.

'My word, somebody's rich!'

'Oh, that's money to help old Grim and his wife,' said Peter. 'Jack brought it, half is from Susie too. We're all going to bring some, Dad. We're so sorry for thinking those awful things about Grim, and for spying on him, when all he was doing was taking care of his wife.'

'Yes. It was a very sad story, wasn't it?' said his father. 'I felt as upset as you did, Peter. I'm glad you want to help. So do I!'

'How can *you* help, Dad?' said Peter, astonished.

'I'll tell you,' said his father. 'You know that little cottage that our old cowman has just left? Well, I'm going to have it done up straightaway, and offer it to old Grim. We need a man to trim the hedges and so on, and if he likes to come to our farm here and work, he can have the cottage and live there with his wife. It's sunny and dry, and she'll be all right there.'

'Dad! Oh Dad! I do love you!' cried Janet, and almost knocked her father over with a great bear-hug. 'We couldn't *bear* to let the Grims go back to that dreadful old place of theirs. Oh, how wonderful to be a grown-up and do things like that!'

'And how wonderful to be young and to belong to the Secret Seven!' said her father. 'You're a set of meddling youngsters, you know, but somehow your heads and hearts are sound, and you do the right thing in the end! Well, I'm glad you found out Grim's secret. Now we can set his mind at rest, and our own too.'

'And we'll give you all our money to help to pay for putting the cowman's old cottage right,' said Jack. 'We meant to help some-how with the money, and we will!'

'Thank you,' said Peter's father. 'Give it

to Peter, and he can give it to me. And let me say this, all of you. You've had many adventures before, you Secret Seven, but I don't think you'll ever have one that has such a satisfactory ending. And one more thing – I'm very, very proud of you all!'

He stood up, smiled round at everyone's pleased face, and went out. Peter looked round, his face glowing.

'Did you hear that, Secret Seven?' he said. 'Did you hear that, Scamper? Three cheers for the Secret Seven! Hip-hip-hip . . .'

'HURRAH!' shouted everyone, and Scamper barked madly. What a curious adventure it had been – and all because of Susie and her aeroplane!

SECRET SEVEN MYSTERY

[1]

Something interesting

Peter and Janet were having breakfast with their father and mother one lovely spring morning. Scamper, their golden spaniel, was lying as usual under the table.

'Dad,' began Peter, but his mother frowned at him.

'Your father is reading the paper,' she said. 'Don't bother him just now!'

His father put down the paper and smiled. 'Do the Secret Seven want to make themselves really useful?' he asked. 'Because I've just read something in my paper that may be right up their street!'

'Oh, Dad – what?' cried Peter, and Janet put down her egg-spoon and looked at him expectantly.

'It's about a girl who's run away from home,' said their father, looking at his paper. 'She stole some money from the desk of her teacher, but when the police went to see her aunt about it, she ran away.'

'But – what can the Secret Seven do about it?' asked Peter, surprised.

'Listen – I'll read you the piece,' said his father, and propped the paper up in front of him. 'Elizabeth Mary Wilhemina Sonning, after being accused of stealing money from the desk of her teacher, was found to be missing from her aunt's house. She took nothing with her but the clothes she was wearing, and is in school uniform and school hat. It is stated that her parents are abroad, and that she has a brother who is at present away in France.'

Peter's father looked up from the paper. 'Now comes the bit that might interest *you*,' he said. 'Elizabeth was seen on the evening of that day in Belling Village, and it is thought that she might be going to her grandmother, who lives not far off.'

'Belling Village! Why that's the next village to ours,' said Janet. 'Oh – you think that the Secret Seven could keep a lookout for Elizabeth! Yes – we could! What's she like?'

'There's a photograph here,' said her father, and passed the paper across. 'Not a very good one – but in her school uniform, which is a help.'

Peter and Janet stared at the picture in the paper. They saw the photograph of a merry, laughing girl a little older than themselves, with a mass of fluffy hair round her face. They thought she looked rather nice.

Though she can't be really, if she stole money and then ran away, thought Janet. She turned to her father. 'Whereabouts in Belling Village does her granny live?'

'It doesn't say, does it?' said her father, reaching for his paper again. 'You'll have to read this evening's paper and see if there are any more details. If the child goes to her granny's she'll be found at once, of course. But if she hides somewhere around the place, you might be able to spot her.'

'Yes. We might,' said Peter. 'The Secret Seven haven't had *anything* interesting to do lately. We'll call a meeting tomorrow. Good thing it's Saturday!'

That evening, Janet sat down to write notices to each of the Secret Seven to call them to a meeting the next day. Each notice said the same things.

> *'Dear S.S. Member,*
> *'A meeting will be held tomorrow*
> *morning, Saturday, at ten sharp, in the*
> *shed. Wear your badges and remember*
> *the password.'*

Peter signed each one, and then he and Janet fetched their bicycles and rode off to deliver the notices, Scamper trotting beside them. They felt pleasantly excited. This new affair might not come to anything – but at least it was something to talk about and to make plans for.

'We'd better buy an evening paper on our way back and see if there's anything else in it about Elizabeth Mary Wilhemina Sonning,' said Peter.

So they stopped at the little newsagent's shop and bought one. They stood outside the shop, eagerly looking through the pages for any mention of the runaway girl. At last they found a small paragraph, headed 'MISSING GIRL'.

'Here it is,' said Peter, thrilled. 'Look, Janet, it says, "Elizabeth Sonning is still missing, and her grandmother states that she has not seen her. Anyone seeing a child whose appearance tallies with the following description is asked to get in touch with the police." Then, see, Janet, there's a good description of her. That's fine – we can read it out to the Seven tomorrow.'

'Good!' said Janet. 'Come on, Scamper – we'll have to bike home pretty fast, so you'll have to run at top speed!'

Scamper puffed and panted after them, his long silky ears flopping up and down as he ran. He wasn't a member of the Secret Seven, but he certainly belonged! No meeting was complete without him.

'What's the password, Peter?' asked Janet, as they put their bicycles away. 'It's ages since we had a meeting.'

'It's a jolly good thing *I* never forget it,' said Peter. 'I shan't tell it to you – but I'll give you a hint. Think of *lamb* – that ought to remind you!'

'Lamb?' said Janet, puzzled. 'Well – it reminds me of sheep, Peter – or Mary had a little lamb – or lamb chops. Which is it?'

'None of them!' said Peter, grinning. 'Have another shot, Janet – and tell me at the meeting tomorrow!'

[2]

Knock – Knock

'Have you remembered the password yet?' asked Peter next morning, when Janet and he were tidying their shed ready for the meeting.

'No, I haven't,' said Janet. 'And I think you might tell me, because you know jolly well I've got to come. I've been thinking of lamb – lamb – lamb for ages, but it doesn't remind me of anything except what I've already told you. Tell me the word, Peter, do!'

'No,' said Peter firmly. 'You're always forgetting. It's time you were taught a lesson. I shan't let you into the meeting unless you remember it. Look – go and ask Mummy if we can have some of those biscuits she made last week.'

'Go yourself,' said Janet, crossly.

'I'm the head of the Secret Seven,' said Peter. 'Obey orders, Janet!'

Janet went off, not feeling at all pleased. She was quite afraid that Peter *wouldn't* let her into the meeting! He was very strict about rules.

She went into the kitchen, but her mother wasn't there. Some lamb chops lay on the table, and Janet looked at them frowning. 'Lamb! Oh dear – whatever ought you to remind me of? I simply can't think! Oh – here's Mummy. Mummy, *may* we have some of your ginger biscuits, please? Oh, what's that you've got? Mint – let me smell it. I love the smell. I wouldn't mind mint scent on my hanky!'

'It's for mint sauce with the chops,' said her mother. 'Now I'll just—'

'Mint sauce! Of *course*! That's the password, Mint sauce! What an idiot I am!' said

Janet. Then she grew serious and looked solemnly at her mother.

'I shouldn't have said the password out loud! We're not supposed to tell a soul. Mummy, don't remember it, will you?'

'What are you gabbling about?' said her mother, and went to get her tin of ginger biscuits. 'Here you are – you can have all of these. I'm making some more for tomorrow.'

'Oh, *thank* you!' said Janet, delighted, and skipped off down the garden with the tin. As she came near the shed she shouted out to Peter.

'Mint sauce, mint sauce, mint sauce!'

'Have you gone mad?' said a cross voice, and Peter looked out of the shed, frowning. 'Shouting out the password for everyone to know! I'm glad you've remembered it at last.'

'Well, Mummy came in with mint to make mint sauce. Wasn't it lucky?' said

Janet. 'Oh, Scamper, you know I've got some ginger biscuits, don't you? I expect there'll be one for you. Peter, it's almost ten o'clock.'

'I know,' said Peter. 'I'm just ready. Are there enough things to sit on? You'll have to sit on that big flowerpot, Janet. The gardener must have taken our seventh box.'

Scamper began to bark. 'That's someone coming already,' said Peter. 'Shut the door, Janet, please. We'll have to ask the password as usual.'

Knock – knock!

'Password!' called Peter.

'Mint sauce!' said two voices.

'Enter!' said Peter, and Janet opened the door. 'Hello, George and Colin. You're very punctual.'

Knock – knock.

'Password!' shouted Peter. A cautious voice came in through the keyhole.

'I've forgotten. But I'm Pam, so you can let me in.'

'No, we can't. You know the rule,' said Peter, sternly.

'Think of lamb chops!' called Janet, before Peter could stop her.

A giggle was heard. 'Oh, yes – of course. MINT SAUCE.'

Janet opened the door, but Peter looked quite cross. 'How dare you remind Pam like that?' he demanded.

'Well, *you* reminded me!' said Janet, indignantly. 'You said, "Think of lamb chops", didn't you?'

'There's someone else coming,' said Peter, changing the subject hurriedly.

Knock – knock! 'Mint sauce,' said two voices.

'Come in!' shouted Peter, and in came Jack and Barbara together. Scamper greeted them with pleasure, and then everyone sat down and looked expectantly at Peter.

'Anything exciting?' asked Jack, eagerly.

'Yes – quite,' answered Peter. 'But what about that awful sister of yours, Jack? Is she anywhere about? This is quite an important meeting.'

'No. She's gone shopping with my mother,' said Jack. 'She doesn't even *know* there's a meeting on. So we're quite safe. She won't come snooping round.'

'Have a ginger biscuit?' asked Janet, and the tin was handed round.

Peter cleared his throat. 'Well, now,' he began, 'it was my father who thought we should inquire into the matter I'm going to tell you about, so you can see it's quite important. It concerns a girl who has run away from her aunt's home, after stealing some money at school. She's been seen near here, at Belling Village, where her grandmother lives – but so far hasn't been to see her granny.'

'Oh – and I suppose it's up to the Secret

Seven to keep a lookout for her – and find her!' said Jack. 'We ought to be able to do *that* all right. What's she like – and what are your plans, Peter?'

'That's just what this meeting is about,' said Peter. 'Now listen!'

[3]

Mostly about Elizabeth

Peter explained everything clearly.

'The girl's name is Elizabeth Mary Wilhemina Sonning,' he said. 'Her parents live abroad, and she is a weekly boarder at school and spends her weekends with an aunt. She has a brother who is away in France. She was accused of stealing money from her teacher's desk, and when the police went to speak to her aunt about it, she ran away.'

'What was she dressed in?' asked Pam.

'School uniform,' said Peter. 'Here's her photograph in it. Ordinary navy school coat, navy felt hat with school band round it, ordinary shoes, and socks. It says here that she wore a grey skirt underneath, with a white blouse – well, really she's dressed just like Janet and Pam and Barbara when they're at school, it seems to me!'

'She might have taken some other clothes with her,' said Jack. 'Her Sunday coat or something.'

'No. Her aunt said that no other clothes were missing – only the ones she went in,' said Peter. 'You may be sure the aunt would look carefully, because it would be difficult to spot the girl if she were not in her school uniform.'

'Where's the description of what she's like?' asked Janet. 'It was in the evening paper last night, Peter.'

'Oh yes. Here it is,' said Peter, and began to read out loud. '"Elizabeth can be recognised by her mass of soft, dark, curly hair, her brown eyes, straight eyebrows, and scar down one arm. She is tall for her age, and strong. She swims well and is fond of horses." Well – there you are – do you think you'd spot her if you saw her?'

'We might,' said Colin, doubtfully. 'But lots of girls have dark, curly hair and brown eyes. If only the girl would wear short sleeves we might spot the scar – but that's the one thing she will certainly hide!'

'How do we set about looking for her?' asked George. 'Do we bike over to Belling Village and hunt all over the place?'

'That's what we've got to discuss,' said Peter. 'I don't actually think that just biking up and down the streets is going to be the slightest good – Elizabeth will be sure to find a hiding-place. She won't wander about in the daytime, I imagine – she'll lie low.'

'Where?' asked Pam.

'How do *I* know?' said Peter, who thought that Pam was sometimes very silly. 'Use your brains, Pam. Where would *you* hide if you ran away from home?'

'In a barn,' said Pam.

'In the woods under a thick bush,' said George.

'Wuff, wuff, wuff-wuff,' said Scamper, wagging his tail.

'What did you suggest – in a *kennel*?' said Peter. 'Thank you, Scamper – quite a good idea of yours.'

Everyone laughed, and Scamper looked pleased.

'I thought it would be sensible if we thoroughly explored Belling Village and round about,' said Peter. 'If Elizabeth has already actually been *seen* in Belling, she must be hiding *some*where near. I expect the police have already hunted pretty well everywhere, but we know better where to look than they do – because we know where *we'd* hide if we wanted to – but they wouldn't. Grown-ups seem to forget the things they did when they were young.'

'Yes, they do,' said George. 'But I *never* shall. I'm determined not to. What about the grandmother, Peter? Should one of us go to see her, do you think? She might have something helpful to say.'

'Yes, I think that's a good idea,' said Peter, considering it.

'Bags *I* don't go,' said Pam, at once. 'I wouldn't know what to say. I should just stand there and look silly.'

'Well, you'd find *that* quite easy,' said Colin, and Pam scowled at him.

'Now just you tell me what you—' she began, but Peter stopped the argument before it began.

'Shut up, you two. Jack and I will go, probably. And listen – there is another thing we might do.'

'What?' asked everyone.

'Well, this girl is fond of horses, it seems. We might go to the two or three stables we know of and see if any girl has been seen hanging around. She might even try to get a job at one.'

'That's a *good* idea,' said Janet, warmly. 'Well – there seems quite a lot we can do, Peter.'

'The next thing is to give each one of us a section of the countryside to hunt,' said Colin. 'It's no good us all going together – for one thing anyone in hiding would hear us coming and lie low. And for another thing we'd never cover all the countryside! What particular places must we search, Peter?'

'Well – you'll use your own common sense about that, of course,' said Peter. 'Anywhere that looks likely – a deserted shack – an empty caravan – a copse – anywhere in the woods where there are thick bushes – barns – sheds – even a hen-house!'

'Wuff, wuff, wuff-wuff,' put in Scamper.

'You mentioned a kennel before, Scamper, old thing,' said Peter. 'We'll leave *you* to examine those. Now, Secret Seven, there

are two hours before dinner. Arrange between yourselves where you're going to
search. Jack and I are going off to the
grandmother's house. Everyone report back
at half-past two – SHARP! Now – get going!'

[4]

Jumble for Mrs Sonning

Peter and Jack went out of the shed together. 'Do you know the address of the grandmother?' asked Jack.

'No, I don't,' said Peter. 'But I know her name is Sonning, the same as the girl's – so I vote we look it up in our telephone book.'

'Good idea,' said Jack. 'We'll get our bikes afterwards.' The two boys went down the path to the garden door, and Peter looked for the telephone book. He found it and began to hunt for the name of Sonning.

'What are you looking for, dear?' asked his mother, coming into the hall. 'Can't you find a number?'

'I was looking for the phone number of

that runaway girl's grandmother,' said Peter. 'But she's not on the phone apparently.'

'But Peter, dear – you can't telephone her house and ask her questions about her granddaughter!' said his mother, quite shocked.

'I wasn't going to, Mother,' said Peter. 'I was going to call there with Jack – but I don't know her address.'

'I know it,' said his mother, surprisingly. 'She often runs jumble sales for Belling Women's Institute, and it was only last week that she wrote and asked me for some old clothes.'

'Some jumble?' said Peter, excited. 'Oh, Mother – what a chance for us! Can't we take some over to her, and say it's from you – and maybe she'll tell us a lot about Elizabeth, her granddaughter. We're looking for her, you know, just as Daddy suggested.'

'Oh dear – you and your Secret Seven!'

said his mother. 'Very well – I'll give you some jumble, and you can say I've sent it by you. But you're to be polite and kind, and if she doesn't want to say a word about Elizabeth, you are NOT to ask questions.'

'All right, Mother. We'll be quite polite, really we will,' said Peter. 'Where's the jumble?'

'In those two boxes,' said his mother. 'I dare say you can strap them on the back of your bicycles if they won't go into your baskets. The address is "Bramble Cottage, Blackberry Lane".'

The two boys hurried off jubilantly with the jumble. 'Wasn't that a bit of luck?' said Peter. 'Come on – we've got a wonderful excuse for calling on the old lady!'

They rode off with Scamper running beside them, panting. They soon came to Belling Village, and asked for Blackberry Lane.

It was a little winding lane, with fields on

one side and a wood on the other. Bramble Cottage was the last house in the lane, a pretty little place with tulips and wall-flowers in the garden, and creepers climbing up the whitewashed walls.

'Here it is,' said Peter, seeing the name on the gate. 'Get your jumble, Jack.'

They carried the two cardboard boxes up the path, and rang the bell beside the green front door. They heard footsteps coming, and then someone in an overall opened the door and looked inquiringly at them.

She couldn't be the grandmother, Peter was certain. She looked a good deal too young.

'We have brought some jumble for Mrs Sonning's sale,' he said. 'May we speak to her, please? I have a message from my mother.'

'Come in,' said the woman, and led the way to a small sitting-room. 'Put the boxes down there, please. You can't see Mrs Sonning – she's in bed, not very well. I'm Miss Wardle, her companion, and *I'll* tell her you brought these.'

'I suppose she's very upset about her granddaughter,' said Peter, plunging in at once. 'My mother was sorry to hear about it too.'

'Ah, yes – the old lady is very troubled,' said Miss Wardle. 'She's so fond of Elizabeth, and is longing for the child to come to her. She doesn't believe all that nonsense about stealing money. Neither do I!'

'Do you know Elizabeth, then?' asked Peter.

'Know her! I've known her since she was so high!' said Miss Wardle. 'And a nicer, more honest, straightforward child I've never seen. A bit of a rascal at times, but none the worse for that. Poor child – I can't bear to think of her hiding away somewhere, afraid to come out.'

'Do you think she's somewhere about

here?' asked Jack. 'She has been seen in the district, hasn't she?'

'Yes – and, what's more, it's my belief she's been here, to this very house!' said Miss Wardle, lowering her voice. 'I haven't told Mrs Sonning about it, it would worry her. But some of my tarts went last night and a meat pie – and a tin of biscuits! And a rug off the backroom sofa!'

This was news indeed! Peter looked at Jack. Elizabeth must certainly be in the district!

'Why do you suppose she won't come to her grandmother and stay with her instead of hiding away?' asked Peter. 'People usually hide when they feel guilty. But you say you don't believe Elizabeth *is* guilty of stealing that money!'

'That's true – I don't,' said Miss Wardle. 'But the pity of it is – the money was found in her chest of drawers! So what are you to believe?'

'Who's that, Emma, who's that?' a voice suddenly called from upstairs. 'Is there any news of Elizabeth?'

'That's Mrs Sonning. You must go,' said Miss Wardle, and ran up the stairs at once.

'Come on,' said Peter to Jack. 'We've got quite a lot of information! And on Monday we'll see if there's any more! I'll find another boxful of jumble, Jack – and we'll bring it to Miss Wardle and see if she has anything more to report – maybe another rug gone, or a pie! Come on, Scamper – we've done well!'

[5]

Pam and Barbara are busy

Now how had the others been getting on?
Well, Pam and Barbara had been having a
very busy time. They had planned to ex-
plore the woods and the fields on the east
side of Belling, while the boys and Janet
explored the rest of the countryside – or as
much as they could!

'There's an old shed on that field, look,'
panted Barbara, as she toiled up a hill on
her bicycle. 'Let's go and see if it looks as if
someone is camping there.'

They left their bicycles by a gate and
climbed into the field. The shed was in good
repair – and the door was locked!

'Hm,' said Pam. 'Locked! I wonder why.
Field sheds aren't usually locked. How can

we look inside, Barbara?'

'There's a tiny window this side,' reported Barbara. 'But too high up to peep through. Let's look through the keyhole.'

There was nothing whatever to see through the keyhole, for the inside of the shed was pitch dark. It would have to be the window or nothing! Pam fetched her bicycle from the gate and proposed to stand on the saddle while Barbara held it steady. She was just about to stand on the saddle when a loud shout made her lose her balance in fright and fall off.

'Hey, you! What are you doing?'

The two girls turned round and saw a farm labourer leading a horse towards them. Pam couldn't think of any excuse but the truth.

'We – we were only just wondering what was in the shed,' she stammered. 'We weren't doing any harm.'

'Well, that's the shed where I lock up my tools,' said the man. 'Little nosy-parkers!

Get off this land before I call the police!'

The girls left that field at top speed, Pam riding her bicycle over the bumpy clods! Gosh – what a cross person!

'We'd better be careful of the next shed we want to look into,' said Pam, as they cycled along. 'Look, there's an empty caravan – see, in that field there. That would be a good place for anyone to hide in. Now for goodness' sake let's be careful this time. I'll keep guard while you look inside. Hurry up!'

Pam stood on guard near the dirty, broken-down old caravan, which looked as if no one had lived in it for years.

Barbara went cautiously up the steps and looked inside.

She beckoned to Pam in excitement.

'Pam! Someone *does* live here! There are a couple of dirty old rugs – or blankets – and a tin mug and plate – do come and look!'

Pam came up the steps too. 'Pooh!' she

said, and held her nose. 'What a DREADFUL smell! Come down, Barbara. You know jolly well you'd never hide in a place like that, nor any other schoolgirl either. I think I'm going to be sick.'

'You're right, I'd rather sleep in a ditch than in there,' said Barbara. 'Don't be sick, Pam. It's not worth it. Come on, let's get on with our job. We want to have plenty to report to the others this afternoon.'

Pam decided not to be sick after all, and they rode on again, keeping a sharp eye out for any kind of hiding-place. But except for a roadman's hut, they saw nothing else that was possible to hide in. They didn't even stop at the little hut, because the roadman himself was there, sitting in it and having some kind of snack.

'What about the woods?' asked Pam, at last. 'There's Thorney-Copse Wood – and it has plenty of thick bushes in it. We might go there. We've still got an hour to look round in.'

So they went to the nearby woods, and left their bicycles beside a tree. 'Now let's be as quiet as possible,' said Pam, in a low voice. 'You go that way, and I'll go this. Whistle twice if you see anything interesting.'

She went quietly in and out of the trees, looking behind any thick bush and even under them. But there was nothing at all interesting or exciting to be seen. Pam found an empty cigarette packet, and Barbara found a dirty handkerchief with J. P. on it, but neither of them felt that they were of any value in the hunt. Now if E.M.W.S. had been marked on the handkerchief, what a thrill!

And then Pam suddenly clutched hold of Barbara, making her jump violently, and hissed in her ear. 'Quiet! Somebody's coming, and it's a girl – look!'

They crept under a thick bush at once, and made little peep-holes through the leaves. Yes, it was a schoolgirl – in navy blue coming down a path towards their bush.

'Keep still – and then we'll follow her!' whispered Pam. 'I bet that's the girl we want!'

The girl's hat was pulled well down over her eyes. She walked boldly up to the bush – and then suddenly fell into it, almost squashing Pam and Barbara. She began to roar with laughter.

'Oh, it's SUSIE. Jack's horrible sister Susie!' cried Barbara, indignantly. 'Get off us, Susie – you've nearly squashed us flat. What did you do that for?'

'Well, you were lying in wait to jump out at me, weren't you?' asked Susie. 'I spotted you crawling into the bush!'

'We were *not* lying in wait for you,' said Pam.

'Well,' said Susie, 'what were you doing then? Come on – you've *got* to tell me!'

[6]

Up at the stables

Pam and Barbara glared at Susie. It was *just* like her to interfere. Pam rubbed her shoulder.

'You've given me a big bruise,' she said. 'And we shan't tell you a thing!'

'It's something to do with the Secret Seven, isn't it?' said Susie. 'Go on, tell me – I know it is. You've got some kind of secret on again, haven't you? Jack has gone off without saying a word to me. Tell me, and I'll help you.'

'Certainly not!' said Pam indignantly. 'We keep our secrets to ourselves!'

'Well – I'll get it out of Jack,' said the irritating Susie, and walked off, tipping her hat over her face once more. 'Goodbye – and don't lie in wait for me again!'

'Now she knows we're in the middle of another excitement,' said Barbara, brushing herself down. 'She's so sharp that I'm sure she'll find out what it is. I do hope we don't keep meeting her looking for Elizabeth too!'

'Time's getting on,' said Pam, looking at her watch. 'We'll just hunt in a few more places, and then we'll have to go home!'

They did quite a lot more hunting, and found an exciting hollow tree which, they decided, would have made a fine place for a runaway girl if she had happened to see it.

'We'll remember it for ourselves, in case we ever need a place like this,' said Barbara. 'Now let's go home. We've nothing to report – except about Susie – but at least we've done our best. I wonder how Colin got on? He was going round the farms and looking into the barns.'

'And George and Janet were going to visit

the riding stables in the district,' said Pam.
'That would be quite a nice job. I love
stables.'

George and Janet thought it was quite a
nice job too. They had looked up the riding
stables in the district, and found that there
were three.

'Belling Riding Stables,' said Janet. 'And
Warner's Riding Stables – and Tiptree's.
We'll go to all three, shall we?'

So off they went on their bicycles, feeling,
as usual, very important to be on Secret
Seven work again. They came to Tiptree's
Stables first. Janet knew the man who ran it,
for he was a friend of her father's.

He was rubbing down a horse and smiled
at Janet and George. 'Well – come to have a
look at my horses?' he said. 'I've a foal in
there, look – Silver Start, she's called, and a
bonny thing she is.'

They admired the lovely little foal. 'I do
wish I worked at a stables,' said Janet,

artfully. 'Do you ever let schoolgirls work here – perhaps in the school holidays, Mr Tiptree?'

The riding master laughed. 'No! I get plenty of help from my wife and two daughters – they're all mad about horses. They do all the work there is to do – I don't need anyone from outside. This is quite a family stables! Why – did you think you'd come and help? Your father has surely got plenty of horses for you to play about with?'

'Well, yes, he has,' said Janet, stroking the little foal. 'I only just wondered if you ever gave jobs to girls – lots of girls I know love horses and wish they could work in a stables.'

'Come on, Janet,' said George, seeing that they could get no useful information from Mr Tiptree. Obviously the runaway girl would not be able to get a job here, even if she wanted one.

'Thank you for showing us the foal,

Mr Tiptree,' said Janet. 'I'll tell my father about her – he'll be interested.'

They rode off again, and George looked at his list of stables. 'We'll go to Warner's Stables next,' he said. 'That's not far from the old granny's house. It might be a good place for Elizabeth Sonning to hide in – or get a job at.'

'I hardly think she'd go anywhere so close, would she?' said Janet. 'She might be recognised. It's more likely she'd go farther off – to Belling Stables, the other side of the village. Still – we'll go to Warner's first.'

They rode up to the stables on the top of the next hill. Below them were spread fields of all kinds and shapes looking like a big patchwork quilt.

Warner's Stables were quite big, and looked busy as they came up to them. Some horses were going out with riders, and others were coming in. Nobody took much notice of the two children.

'Let's have a snoop round,' said Janet. 'And if we see any stable-girls, we'll have a good look at them.'

'Wouldn't Elizabeth have to wear riding things if she wanted a job at a stable?' said George. 'We know that she was wearing her school clothes when she left – she took no others.'

'Well – she might have borrowed some at the stables,' said Janet. 'Though that's rather unlikely, I think. Look – there's a stable-girl – see – cleaning out that stable.'

They stood and stared at the girl. Her back was towards them, and she was doing her job well. She turned round to fetch something, and at once they saw that it was not Elizabeth.

'Far too big!' said Janet, disappointed. 'Look – there are two stable-boys over there. Let's go and talk to them – we may learn something, you never know.'

[7]

Tom has some news

George and Janet made their way between the horses and their riders to where the two stable-boys were. One was carrying a great load of straw on his back. The other was helping a small girl down from a pony. They took no notice of George and Janet.

'Hallo, Janet!' said the small girl, and Janet turned in surprise. It was Hilda, a little girl who went to her school, and was two years below her.

'Hallo, Hilda,' said Janet, feeling pleased to see her. Now she could pretend she was with her, and it wouldn't matter that she and George were not in riding clothes. Everyone would think they had come to meet Hilda.

'Thank you, Tom,' said Hilda to the boy

who had helped her down. He took the pony off to a nearby stable. Hilda followed him, accompanied by Janet and George.

'I like the other boy best,' Hilda said. 'He talks to me, but this one won't. Come and see me give my pony some sugar. He's a darling.'

They walked over to the stable with her, following Tom and the pony. The other lad had gone into the same stable with his straw, and was now spreading it on the floor of a stall. He whistled as he worked, and had a merry look in his eye.

'You talk to this boy, and I'll talk to the other one,' said George, in a low voice to Janet. 'Talk to Hilda too – find out if any new girl is here helping in any way – or if she has seen any strange girl wandering about, watching, as we are doing.'

'Right,' said Janet, and went to Tom and Hilda.

'It must be fun working with horses,' she

said to the boy, who was now fastening the pony to the wall. He nodded.

'Not bad,' he said.

'It's funny that so many more girls ride than boys,' went on Janet. 'I can't see a single boy here except you, and the other stable-boy. Are there any others?'

'No,' said the boy. 'Just us two.' He began to clean out the stall next to the little pony, turning his back on Hilda and Janet. Janet thought he was rather rude. So did Hilda.

'He's like that,' she whispered to Janet. 'The other boy, Harry, doesn't mind telling you anything. He's talking to George as if he's known him for years.'

So he was. George was getting on very well indeed!

'Do they have many stable-girls here?' George asked, when he had a good chance. The burly fellow shook his head.

'Only one – and she's over there. One came the other day to ask for a job, but Mr Warner turned her down at once. Why, she wasn't any bigger than you! And yet she said she could handle this big cob over there.'

George pricked up his ears. He wasn't interested in the cob, but he was interested in this girl who had come for a job. Could it have been Elizabeth?

'What was she like?' he asked. Harry called across to the other stable-boy.

'Hey, Tom – what was that girl like who came and asked for a job the other day?'

'Was she brown-eyed?' asked George, eagerly. 'Had she masses of dark, fluffy hair? And did you notice if she had a scar down one of her arms?'

The stable-boy swung round sharply and stared at George. 'What girl's that?' he asked. 'Is she a friend of yours?'

'No, not exactly,' said George. 'It's – er – well, it's just someone we're looking out for. Do tell me, was this girl like my description of her?'

'I didn't see her,' said Tom, much to Janet's and George's disappointment. 'I wasn't here the day she came.'

'Oh, no – that's right,' said Harry. 'Well, I know she hadn't got dark hair – she had yellow hair, and she was lively as a monkey. Very cross too, when Mr Warner turned her down. She couldn't have been your friend.'

'I saw a girl like the one you described when I was in Gorton the other day,' said Tom suddenly. 'Mass of fluffy brown hair, you said, didn't you – and a scar down one arm.'

'Did you? Did you *really* see her?' cried Janet, coming up, looking thrilled. Now they were really getting warm! 'How did you manage to see her scar?'

'Oh – she sat in a tea-shop, and it was hot there – so she took off her coat,' said Tom. 'I saw her scar then.

'But hadn't she a long-sleeved school blouse on?' asked Janet, surprised.

'Maybe. But her sleeves must have been rolled up if so,' said Tom, and bent to his work again.

'Tom – this is really very important,' said George, joining in. 'Could you tell us anything she said – did she speak to you?'

'She said she was going to catch a train to London and see if she could fly to France to join a brother of hers,' said Tom, to Janet's and George's surprise and excitement. Why, the girl *must* have been Elizabeth, then. A scar on her arm – and a brother in France! There was no doubt about it!

'Tom! I want you!' called a voice, and Mr Warner looked into the stable. 'Come and show this child how to saddle her horse.'

Tom went off, and Janet and George looked at one another, delighted. 'Well – we've got something to report to the meeting this afternoon!' said Janet. 'Come on, George – we needn't stay here any longer.'

[8]

Another meeting

Everyone was early for the two-thirty meeting, and the password was muttered five times as Janet and Peter opened and shut the door of the shed. Scamper barked a welcome to everyone. Then the door was locked and the meeting began.

'I hope everyone has something to report,' said Peter. 'I'll begin with my report. Well, Jack and I went to the grandmother's house, but the old lady wasn't well, so we didn't see her. We didn't find it difficult to ask questions, and her companion was quite friendly.'

'That was a bit of luck!' said George.

'It was,' said Peter. 'We learnt quite a few things – for instance, that Elizabeth is

definitely hiding somewhere in the district –
not far from her granny's, I should think –
because she has got into the house at night
and taken pies and things, and an old rug!'

George and Janet looked astonished.
'But, Peter— ' began George and Janet
together. Peter frowned. 'Please don't inter-
rupt,' he said. 'You and Janet can have your
say in a minute. Well, as I was saying – the
old lady's companion, Miss Wardle – told
us quite a lot about Elizabeth, and said that
she was a very nice, straightforward girl.'

'She can't be!' interrupted Pam. 'You
can't call a thief straightforward! She was
only just *saying* that!'

'Be quiet,' said Peter, exasperated. 'The
point I'm trying to make is that there's no
doubt that Elizabeth is hiding somewhere
near her grandmother's – and getting food
from there. And she'll do that at night as
often as she needs food! I suggest that we go
and watch one night, and see if we can catch

her. Jack and I are going to take some more jumble to the grandmother's on Monday, and if Elizabeth has been getting into the house again, we could perhaps watch that night.'

'Yes. Jolly good idea!' said Pam, Barbara, and Colin. George and Janet said nothing, but looked meaningly at one another.

'Well, that's my report – mine and Jack's,' said Peter. 'What about you, Colin?'

'Nothing to report at all,' said Colin, in a rather apologetic tone. 'I examined about six sheds, all kinds of barns, and wandered over a whole caravan colony the other side of Belling Hill – but didn't find out a thing. Not a thing. I'm sorry, Peter.'

'That's all right,' said Peter. 'You and Pam, Barbara – what's your report?'

'Well, nothing much, either,' said Barbara. 'We looked in a locked shed – or tried to – and got turned off by a man with a horse. And we found a terribly smelly old caravan with a rug inside and a tin cup and plate. And we hunted all through Thorney-Copse Wood, looking into and under bushes.'

'And that awful sister of Jack's was there, too,' said Pam. 'We saw her coming along, dressed in the same uniform as we wear – navy blue coat and hat – and we thought it might be the runaway girl, so we hid in a bush – and Susie jumped right into it on purpose and fell on top of us – you should see the bruise I've got!'

'So *that's* why Susie was pestering the life out of me at dinner to find out what the Secret Seven are up to!' said Jack. 'You *are* a couple of idiots to make her think there is something up, you two. Now I shan't have a moment's peace. Susie is bound to find out what we're after – she's as sharp as a needle.'

'She certainly is,' said Peter, who had a healthy respect for Susie's sharpness. 'I wouldn't be a bit surprised if she's not snooping outside somewhere now, listening for all she's worth.'

'Scamper would bark,' began Janet – and just at that very moment Scamper *did* bark as a face looked in at the window of the shed! It was Susie, of course.

'Hello, Secret Seven,' she called. 'I *thought* you'd be here, Jack. I know what you're all up to. I found your newspaper cutting! Ha, ha.'

Peter looked furiously at Jack. 'Do you mean to say you left that newspaper report about?' he said.

'That's right, tick him off!' said the annoying Susie, pressing her face closer to the window. 'Hey, you do look a lot of sweetie-pies sitting down there. Shall I tell you my news of Elizabeth Mary Wilhemina Sonning?'

Jack leapt up in a fury, flung open the door, and raced out with Scamper at his heels. The others went to the door.

Susie was a fast runner. She was running out of the gate, laughing, before Jack was half-way there. He knew it was no good chasing after her. He went back to the shed, red in the face.

'Do you suppose she heard what we were all saying?' asked Jack. Peter shook his head.

'No. Scamper would have barked. Susie could only just that moment have come. I must say it's very annoying. Now Susie will be hunting too. Bother! If she finds Elizabeth before we do, I shall be jolly furious.'

'She won't,' said George, bursting to tell what he had heard from Tom the stable-boy. 'You just wait till you hear what Janet and I have to report.'

Reports and plans

'Give your report, George and Janet,' said Peter. 'It sounds as if it may be an important one.'

'It is,' said Janet, proudly. 'You begin, George.'

'Well,' began George, 'Janet and I went to Tiptree Stables first, but as they don't employ anyone there except their own family, we knew Elizabeth wouldn't have got a job there. So we left at once and went on to Mr Warner's stables.'

'And we saw a stable-girl there, but she was much too big to be Elizabeth,' put in Janet.

'Then we saw two stable-boys – one a big, burly fellow called Harry, and the other smaller, called Tom. He was a bit surly, we thought, but Harry wasn't. He was nice. We asked him if any girl had been asking for a job at Mr Warner's, and one had, but she had yellow hair not brown, so we knew that was no good.'

'And when we told Harry what the girl was like that we wanted, the other boy, Tom, who was listening, suddenly said that *he* had seen a girl like the one we were describing – and she even had a scar down one arm!' cried Janet unable to resist joining in.

'What!' cried everyone, and sat up straight.

'This *is* news,' said Peter, delighted. 'Go on, George. Where had he seen Elizabeth – because it must be her if the description tallies.'

'He said he met her in a tea-shop in Gorton – that's not very far from here, is it? She was having tea, I suppose. It was hot and she had her coat off – that's how he noticed the scar down one arm. She talked to him.'

'What did she say?' demanded Peter, his eyes shining.

'She told him she was going to London to see if she could get a plane to fly to France to see her brother,' said Janet. 'She did really! So it *must* have been Elizabeth, mustn't it?'

'Yes. Of course it must,' said Peter, and the others nodded their heads. A brother in France – a scar on one arm – it could *only* be Elizabeth.

'Well, now you see why Janet and I don't think that Elizabeth is hiding anywhere in the district,' said George. 'She's probably hiding somewhere in London, trying to find out about planes.'

'Well – can you answer this question then, if that's so,' said Peter, looking suddenly puzzled. 'If Elizabeth is in London, waiting to fly to France, who is it who is taking pies and a rug from her grandmother's house at night?'

There was a deep silence. Everyone looked at Peter, even Scamper.

'I hadn't thought of that,' said Janet. 'Well, of course, George and I didn't know anything about the pies till you told us in your report, Peter. Bother! One of our reports is wrong somehow. If Elizabeth is hanging round her granny's house at night, she can't be going to fly to France!'

'She might have found that she hadn't enough money to get to London and buy a seat on a plane,' said Jack. 'She might have changed her mind and gone to Belling, after all. She might even have hoped to get money from her grandmother's house. After all, if she had stolen once, she could easily do so again.'

'That's true,' said Peter. 'Yes – I think you're right, Jack. She may have made that plan at the beginning and then found she hadn't enough money – and so she came to this district. We know she was seen somewhere about here.'

There was another silence. The Seven were trying to sort things out in their minds. 'What about that girl who came to ask Mr Warner for a job – the one Harry told you about,' said Janet to George. 'He said she had golden hair, didn't he? Well, I suppose she might have had it dyed, mightn't she – I mean, that *might* have been Elizabeth, after all. I know my auntie once had her hair dyed golden when it was brown. So Elizabeth could have done the same, couldn't she?'

Nobody knew very much about hair being dyed, and Peter made up his mind that the next thing to do was to go and interview the two stable-boys himself. They might be able to tell him something they hadn't thought of telling Janet or George.

'I shall go and see those boys,' he said. 'What are they like to look at?'

'I told you Harry was big and burly, and the other smaller,' said George. 'They've both got dark hair, rather untidy. They ought to exchange riding-breeches too – Harry's are too small for him, and Tom's are too large! Wasn't it a bit of luck Tom meeting Elizabeth at Gorton – now we know for certain she must be somewhere about, still wearing her school things.'

'Well, she's *got* to be somewhere near, or she couldn't raid her granny's house at night,' said Peter. 'Now, what do we do next? Tomorrow's Sunday, we can't do anything then. It will have to be Monday after school.'

'You and I will go to old Mrs Sonning's with some more jumble,' said Jack, 'and find out the latest news from *that* quarter.'

'And after that we'll go and see the stable-boys,' said Peter. 'The others can come too, so that it won't seem too noticeable, us asking questions. Meet here at five o'clock on Monday. Well – I *hope* we're on the trail – but it's not very easy at the moment!'

[10]

Miss Wardle has more news

Sunday passed rather slowly.

When Peter and Janet came back from morning church, Peter had an idea.

'Janet – George and I are going to take some more jumble to old Mrs Sonning to-morrow, you remember – to make an excuse for asking about Elizabeth again – so shall we hunt up some? What sort of things does Mother give for jumble? Old clothes mostly, I suppose.'

'Yes. But we can't give away any of our clothes without asking her,' said Janet. 'And she would want to know why we were doing it – she'd guess it was an excuse to go to old Mrs Sonning again, and she might not approve.'

'That's just what I was thinking,' said Peter. 'I know – let's turn out our cupboards and see if there's anything we can find that would do for jumble.'

They found plenty! It was astonishing what a lot of things they had which they had quite forgotten about and never used.

'Two packs of snap cards,' said Peter. 'A game of snakes and ladders – we've never even *used* it, because we always preferred our old game. And look here – a perfectly new ball! Shall we give that?'

'Well, jumble isn't really supposed to be *new* things,' said Janet. 'Let's give our old ball instead. And look, here are my old sandals I thought I'd left at the seaside! I can't get into them now – *they* can go.'

In the end they had quite a big box full of jumble and felt very pleased with themselves. They longed for Monday to come!

It came at last, and then there was morning school to get through, and afternoon school as well. They raced home to tea and were down in the shed just before five o'clock. All the Seven were there, very punctual indeed!

'Good,' said Peter, pleased. 'Well, Jack and I will bike to Bramble Cottage, and see if we can get any more news out of Miss Wardle, the companion, or Mrs Sonning, the granny. The rest of you can bike up to Warner's Stables and wait for us there. Chat to the stable-boys all you can. We'll join you later.'

They all set off, Peter with a neat box of jumble tied to the back of his bicycle. They parted at the top of Blackberry Lane, and Jack and Peter went down the winding road, while the others rode up the hill to where Warner's Stables were, right at the top.

Peter and Jack left their bicycles at the gate of Bramble Cottage and went to the front door. They knocked, hoping that Miss

Wardle would come, not old Mrs Sonning. Mrs Sonning might not be so willing to talk about Elizabeth as Miss Wardle was!

Thank goodness it was Miss Wardle who opened the door again. She seemed quite pleased to see them.

'Well now – don't say you've been kind enough to bring us some *more* jumble!' she said. 'Mrs Sonning was *so* pleased with the boxes you brought on Saturday. I'll give her these – she's still in bed, dear old lady.'

'Oh, I'm sorry,' said Peter. 'Hasn't she heard any more of her granddaughter?'

'Not a word,' said Miss Wardle. 'The police say she seems to have disappeared completely – and yet she came here again last night – *and* the night before!'

This was indeed news! 'Did she?' asked Peter eagerly. 'Did you see her? Did she leave a note?'

'No. Not a note, not even a sign that she was here,' said Miss Wardle, 'except that

more food was gone. How she got in beats
me. Every door and window I made fast
myself. She must have got a key to the side-
door. That's the only one with no bolt.'

'What do the police say about that?'
asked Jack.

'Nothing,' said Miss Wardle, rather indignantly. 'It's my belief they think I'm
making it up, they take so little notice.
Why don't they put a man to watch the
house at night – they'd catch the poor child
then, and what a relief it would be to the old
lady to know she was safe!'

'They probably *do* put a man to
watch,' said Peter, 'but I expect Elizabeth
knows some way into the house that they
don't. I bet she knows if there's a policeman about – and where he is and everything. *I* would! Why don't you watch,
Miss Wardle?'

'What? Watch every door and window?'
said the companion. 'Nobody could do

that. And I'm not one to be able to keep awake all night, even if I had to.'

'Well – we'd better go,' said Peter. 'I *do* hope Elizabeth is soon found. It must be awful hiding away in some cold, lonely place all by herself, not daring to come home because she feels ashamed.'

They said goodbye and went. 'Well,' said Peter, as soon as they were out of the front gate, 'I know what *I'm* going to do tonight! I'm going to hide somewhere in the garden here! I bet I'll see Elizabeth if she comes – but I shan't tell the police. I'll try and get her to go and tell everything to her granny!'

'Good idea! I'll come too!' said Jack, thrilled. 'Let's go up to the stables now and find the others. I bet they'll want to come and watch as well!'

[11]

Tom – and a bit of excitement

Peter and Jack saw the others as soon as they pushed open the tall double-gate and went into the big stable-yard. They had evidently been sent to fetch hay and straw, and looked very busy indeed, carrying it over their shoulders. The two stable-boys were there as well, helping.

'Hallo, Peter – hallo, Jack!' called Janet. 'Aren't we busy? We're having a lovely time. Mr Warner said we could take the ponies down to the field later on, with Harry and Tom, the stable-boys.'

'Good. I'll come too, with Jack,' said Peter, pleased. He loved anything to do with horses, and often helped old Jock, the horseman, in his father's farm-stables.

He went over to the two stable-boys. Harry grinned at him, but Tom just nodded. Peter looked at him keenly. So this was the boy who had actually seen Elizabeth!

'Hey – I hear you saw that girl, Elizabeth Sonning, at Gorton the other day,' began Peter. 'That's very interesting. The police haven't found her yet – I should think her grandmother must be feeling ill with worry, wouldn't you?'

'What about the girl, then?' said Tom, in a gruff voice. 'I reckon she must be feeling pretty awful too.'

'Well, if she stole that money, she deserves to feel awful,' said Peter. 'The funny thing is that Miss Wardle, who is the old lady's friend, says Elizabeth is an awfully nice girl, straightforward as anything! Here – let me help you with that saddle.'

'Thanks,' said Tom. 'I feel interested in that girl – seeing her in Gorton just by chance. I reckon she's in France by now. She said she wanted to go to her brother.'

'Well, she's *not* in France,' said Peter, struggling with the heavy saddle. 'She goes each night to her granny's house and takes things. Miss Wardle told me that. She says she can't *think* how Elizabeth gets into the house – everything's locked and fastened. She thought maybe the girl might have a key to the side-door, which has no bolts.'

Jack joined in then. 'And we thought we'd go and watch the house ourselves tonight,' he said. 'We're sure *we* should see her getting in, if she comes in the dark – and we'd try and get her to go and talk to her old granny, who loves her. We hate to think of a girl camping out somewhere all alone, feeling miserable.'

'Are you really going to watch tonight?' said Tom, sounding surprised. Peter nodded. He hadn't wanted Jack to tell a Secret Seven plan to the stable-boy – that was really *silly* of him, thought Peter, and gave him a stern frown, which startled Jack very much.

'Well, if you're going to watch the house, I'd like to come too,' said Tom, most surprisingly. 'I bet *I* could see anyone creeping into a house at night. I'll come with you.'

Peter hesitated. He wanted to say that Tom could certainly *not* come! But how could he prevent him if he wanted to? It was just a nice little adventure to him, and possibly a chance to show how clever he was at spotting anyone breaking into a house!

'All right,' he said, at last. 'We shall be there at half-past ten. I'll give an owl-hoot when we arrive – and if you're there, hoot back.'

'I'll be there,' said Tom. 'And I suppose a policeman or two will, as well! Well, you stick up for me if I get seen by the police, and say I'm a friend of yours, not a burglar!'

'All right,' said Peter, wishing more than ever that Jack hadn't said so much. 'Do we take the ponies down to the fields now?'

Apparently they did, and a long trail of children riding or leading ponies went over the hill and down to the fields, bright in the evening sun.

After they had safely fastened in the tired ponies, the Seven, with Tom and Harry, walked back to the stables. Tom looked tired and spoke very little. Harry cracked jokes and slapped the other stable-boy on the back several times. Peter whispered to Tom when he had a chance.

'Don't forget the owl-hoot!'

Tom nodded and turned away. The children shouted goodbye and fetched their bicycles, riding them down the hillpath.

In the distance they saw someone climbing over a stile – someone with a suitcase – someone in a navy blue coat and hat – someone who looked round and then, seeming scared, ran hurriedly down the road.

'Look!' said Colin, pointing. 'Is that Elizabeth – with a suitcase, too! Quick, let's follow!'

They rode along the path, bumping up and down as they went, for it was very rough. They came to the stile. By it lay something white.

Janet picked it up. 'A handkerchief!' she said. 'LOOK! It's got E in the corner, embroidered in green! It *was* Elizabeth! Her hiding-place *is* somewhere near here. Quick, let's follow her.'

They lifted their bicycles over the stile into the road and looked to see if they could spy a running figure in navy blue.

'There she is – at the corner – by that old cottage!' shouted George. 'If only we can get her to be friends and come with us! Ring your bells, all of you, so that she'll hear us coming!'

[12]

How very annoying!

The whole Seven cycled as fast as they could after the disappearing figure in navy blue, ringing their bells loudly to attract her attention.

The figure reached the corner, and vanished round it. When they came to it, the girl was nowhere to be seen. The Seven dismounted from their bicycles and looked at one another.

'Wherever has she gone? She's nowhere down the road!' said Janet. 'She must have slipped into some hiding-place. But I can't see any near by.'

'Yes, look – there's that ruined old cottage,' said Colin, pointing. 'Can't you see it – among that little thicket of trees. I bet she's there!'

'We'll go and look,' said George, and, putting their bicycles beside the hedge, they squeezed through a gap and ran over to the old stone cottage. It had very little roof left, and there were only two rooms below and one above. A broken stone stairway went up in one corner to the room above.

'There's nobody here!' said Pam, surprised. 'Oh, but look – there's an old stone stairway. Perhaps she's up there!'

George ran up – and gave a shout. 'The girl isn't here – but her suitcase is! And it's got E.M.W.S. on it! It *was* Elizabeth we saw!'

Everyone tore up the stairs in a hurry. They looked at the cheap little suitcase on the dirty floor. Yes – it certainly had E.M.W.S. printed on it in black.

'Elizabeth Mary Wilhemina Sonning,' said Barbara, touching the initials. 'But where *is* Elizabeth?' she called loudly. 'Elizabeth! Where are you?'

There was no reply. 'That's odd,' said

Janet. 'There really isn't anywhere for her to hide here. Why did she throw her case up these stairs and then rush away. She might guess we'd find it. Where *is* she? ELIZA-BETH!'

'I'm going to open the case,' said Peter. 'I feel there's something peculiar about all this. I hope it isn't locked.'

It wasn't. It snapped open easily enough. The Seven crowded round to look inside. One small box was there, and nothing else. It was tied up with string.

'Perhaps this is the money she stole!' said Colin. 'Gosh – look! It's got "THE MONEY" printed on it in big letters. Open the box, Peter.'

Peter undid the string and opened the box. Inside was a smaller one, also tied with string. He undid that, and inside found once again another box. He looked puzzled. It seemed strange to put money inside so many boxes!

He opened the third box – and inside that was a card, laid on its face. Peter picked it up and turned it over. He stared at it as if he couldn't believe his eyes!

'What does it say? What does it say?' cried Pam, trying to see.

Peter flung it down on the floor and stamped on it, looking very angry. 'It says "*Lots and lots of love from Susie!*" OH! I'd like to slap her! Making us chase after her – leaving that silly hanky by the stile – and making us undo all those boxes!'

The Secret Seven were very, very angry, especially Jack. 'How *dare* she play a trick like that!' he said. 'Just wait till I get home. I'll have something to say to her!'

'Where's she gone?' said Barbara. 'I didn't see her after we turned the corner. She must have had her bicycle hidden some- where here.'

'She planned it all very well,' said George. 'I must say she's jolly clever. Gosh – I really *did* think we'd got hold of Elizabeth that time!'

'Susie must have laughed like anything when she printed the initials E.M.W.S. on that cheap old suitcase,' said Jack. 'I recognise it now – it's been up in our loft for ages.'

'Well, come on – let's get home,' said Janet. 'I'm tired of talking about Susie.'

They left the little ruined cottage and rode away. Peter began to arrange the night's meeting with George, Jack, and Colin. The girls were sad that they could not come too.

'You always leave us out of these night adventures,' complained Janet. 'I do so wish we were coming. It will be so exciting to wait in that dark garden – let me see – there will be five of you counting that boy Tom – though I really do think it's a pity to have him, too.'

'There may be a policeman or two as well,' said George. 'I vote we get there before they do – or they'll get rather a shock when they hear a whole collection of people taking up their positions here and there in the garden!'

Everyone laughed. 'Don't you DARE to let anything out to Susie about tonight,' Peter warned Jack. 'We can't have her ruining everything. I do wonder how Elizabeth gets into the house. She must have an extra key.'

They arranged to meet at ten past ten at the corner and bicycle all together to Belling. 'We'll hide our bikes under the nearby hedge and get into the garden at the back,' planned Peter. 'Remember to hoot if there's any danger.'

'This is awfully exciting,' said Jack. 'I only hope Susie doesn't hear me getting up and going downstairs.'

'Jack – if you do anything silly so that Susie follows you, I'll dismiss you from the Secret Seven!' said Peter – and he REALLY meant it!

[13]

Waiting and watching

That night Peter, Jack, George and Colin slipped silently out of their houses. Jack was very much afraid that Susie might hear him, but when he put his ear to her door, he could hear gentle little snores. Good – she was asleep! He remembered Peter's threat to dismiss him from the Secret Seven if he wasn't careful about Susie, and he felt very glad to hear those snores!

The boys met together and then cycled quickly over to the grandmother's house in Belling. They met nobody at all, not even a policeman, and were very thankful. The four of them dismounted quietly and put their bicycles into the hedge beyond Bramble Cottage. The cottage was in complete darkness.

'The only person to hoot is *me*,' whispered Peter. 'If we all hoot when we hear or see something interesting or suspicious, it would sound as if the garden was *full* of owls – and any policeman would be most suspicious!'

'All right,' whispered back George. 'Can we choose our own hiding-places? What about two of us going to hide in the garden at the front of the house, and two at the back?'

'No – two at the back, one in the front – you, Colin – and one at the side where the side-door is,' said Peter, in a low voice. 'Don't forget that Miss Wardle said she thought Elizabeth might have a key to that door – and there are no bolts there on the inside!'

'Oh, yes!' said Jack. 'I'll go and hide in the hedge beside the garden door, Peter. There isn't any door on the fourth side. We shall be watching every door there is – and every window.'

'It's very dark,' said Peter, looking up at the sky. 'There's no moon, and it's a cloudy night, so there are no stars either. We shall have to keep our ears wide open, because it may be pretty difficult to see anything.'

'Our eyes will soon get used to the darkness,' said Colin. 'Hey – listen, what's that?' He clutched at Peter and made him jump.

A slight noise came from near by, and then a shadow loomed up. A voice spoke. 'It's me – Tom. I was waiting here, and I heard you. Where are you hiding?'

They told him. 'Well, I think *I'll* climb up a tree,' said Tom, in a low voice. 'That will be a very good place to watch from – or listen from! I don't think any policemen are about. I've been here for some time.'

'Hoot if you hear anyone coming,' Peter reminded him. 'I'll hoot back. But only you or I will hoot.'

'I'll find a tree to climb,' whispered Tom. 'See – that one over there, near the wall. I shall have a good view from there – if only the clouds clear and the stars shine out!'

The four went to find their own hiding-places, feeling pleasantly excited. This *was* fun! They heard Tom climbing his tree. Then there was silence. Peter was snuggled into a bush, from where he could keep good watch.

A sudden screech made everyone jump, and their hearts beat fast. Whatever was it? Then a white shadow swept round the dark garden, and everyone heaved a sigh of relief.

Only a barn-owl! thought Peter. Gosh – it made me jump. Good thing it doesn't hoot, only screeches – or we would all of us have thought that someone was coming!

Nothing happened for a while – then a low, quavering hoot came across the garden. 'Hoo! Hoo-hoo-hoo-hoooooooo!'

That's Tom! thought Peter, and he and the others in hiding stiffened, and listened hard, trying to see through the darkness.

Then someone brushed by Peter's bush and he crouched back in fright. He heard a little cough – a man's cough. It must be a policeman who had come along so quietly that no one but Tom had heard him. Peter waited a few seconds till he was sure that the man had found a hiding-place, and then he hooted too.

'Hoo! Hoo-hoo-hoo-hooooooo!'

Now everyone must guess that at least one policeman was in the garden! Peter's heart began to thump. Suddenly things seemed very strange and very exciting – all the dark shadows around, and so many people waiting! He half hoped that Elizabeth would not come to her granny's house that night. It would be so frightening for her to be surrounded suddenly by complete strangers!

Then suddenly he stared in amazement. Was that a *light* he saw in one of the upstairs rooms of the house? A light like that made by a torch? Yes – it was! He could see the beam moving here and there behind the drawn curtains!

Elizabeth must be there – she must have got in somehow, in spite of everyone watching! Or could it be Miss Wardle creeping about with a torch? No – surely she would switch on a light!

Peter gave a hoot again. 'Hoooo! Hoo-hoo-hoo-hoooooooo!' That would make certain that everyone was on guard. If Elizabeth had got in, then she would have to get out – and surely one of them would see her!

The light in the upstairs room disappeared – and reappeared again in another room. Peter thought it was the kitchen. Perhaps the hungry runaway girl was looking for food again?

HOW HAD she got in? But, more important still – where was she going to come out?

[14]

A real mystery!

The light from the torch inside the house moved here and there. Then it disappeared completely, as if it had been switched off. All the watchers listened, and strained their eyes in the darkness. Now Elizabeth would be leaving the house, and they must stop her. What door – or what window – would she creep from?

Nothing happened. No door opened. No window creaked or rattled. For ten minutes the watchers stood silent and tense. Then a man's voice called from somewhere in the garden.

'Will! Seen anyone?'

To Peter's intense surprise another man's voice answered. 'No. Not a thing. The kid must be still in the house. We'll knock up Miss Wardle and search.'

So there were *two* policemen in the garden then! How very quiet the other one had been! The boys were most surprised. *Now* what should they do? They watched the policemen switch on torches and heard them go to the front door of the house.

Peter hooted once more, and the others, realising that he wanted them, left their hiding-places and came cautiously to find him. Tom slid down the tree and joined them too.

'The policemen didn't hear or see anyone – any more than we did!' said Peter. 'We could only have seen what they saw – a light in the downstairs of the house. Tom, did *you* see anything else?'

'Not a thing,' said Tom. 'Look – I'll slip off, I think. The police don't know me, and they might wonder what I'm doing here with you. So long!'

He disappeared into the night and left the four boys together. They went near to the front door, at which the policemen had rung a minute ago, keeping in the dark shadows. The door was being opened cautiously by a very scared Miss Wardle, dressed in a long green dressing-gown, her hair in pins.

'Oh – it's you!' the boys heard her say to the police. 'Come in. I'm afraid I was asleep, although I said I'd try and keep awake tonight. Do you want me to go and see if anything is taken?'

'Well, Miss Wardle, we know that *someone* was in your house just now,' said one of the policemen. 'We saw the light of a torch in two rooms. One of us would like to come in and search, please – the other will stay out here in case the girl – if it is the girl – tries to make a run for it. We haven't seen her come out – or go in either for that matter! But we did see the light of her torch.'

'Oh, I see. Well, come in, then,' said Miss Wardle. 'But please make no noise, or you'll scare the old lady. Come into the kitchen – I can soon tell if food is gone again.'

The policeman disappeared into the cottage with Miss Wardle, leaving the other man on guard in the garden. The four boys watched from the safety of the shadows. Surely Elizabeth must be in the house? She couldn't have left by any door or window without being seen or heard! They watched lights going on in each room, as Miss Wardle and the policeman searched.

After what seemed like a very long time, they heard voices in the hall. Miss Wardle came to the door with the policeman.

'Nothing to report, Will,' said the policeman to the man left on guard. 'Nobody's in the house. Miss Wardle even went into the old lady's room to make sure the girl hadn't crept in there, feeling that she was cornered.'

'Well – nobody's come *out* of the house,' said Will, sounding surprised. 'Has anything been taken?'

'Yes – more food. Nothing else,' said the first policeman. 'Strange, isn't it? How could anyone have got in under our very eyes and ears – taken food – and got out again without being heard or seen going away? Well – thanks, Miss Wardle. Sorry to have been such a nuisance for nothing. How that girl – and it *must* be the girl – gets in and out like this beats me. And where she's hiding beats me too. We've combed the countryside for her! Well – her brother's coming over to this country tomorrow – not that *he* can do much, if we can't!'

The police departed. The front door shut. The light went off in the hall, and then one appeared upstairs. Then that went out too. Miss Wardle was presumably safely in bed again.

'What do you make of it, Peter?' whispered Jack. 'Peculiar, isn't it?'

'Yes. I can't understand it,' said Peter. 'I mean – there were us four hiding here – and two policemen – and Tom up the tree – and yet not one of us saw Elizabeth getting in and out – and not one of us even *heard* her.'

'And yet she must have come here, into this garden,' said Jack. 'She broke in somewhere – or unlocked a door – she even put on her torch in the house to see what she could take – and then she got out again, with us all watching and listening – and disappeared. No – I don't understand it either.'

'Come on – let's go home and sleep on it,' said Peter. 'I feel quite tired now, with all the waiting and watching – and the excitement – and now the disappointment. Poor Elizabeth – what must she be feeling, having to scrounge food at night, and hide away in the daytime? She must be very miserable.'

'Well – maybe her brother can help,' said Colin. 'He'll be here tomorrow. Come on – I'm going home!'

[15]

Crosspatches

The four boys belonging to the Secret Seven, overslept the next morning. They were so tired from their long watch the night before! Janet was cross when Peter wouldn't wake, because she was longing to know what happened!

'Gosh – I'll be terribly late for school,' groaned Peter, leaping out of bed. 'You might have woken me before, Janet.'

'Well, I squeezed a sponge of cold water over you, and yelled in your ear, and pulled all the clothes off!' said Janet indignantly. 'And Scamper barked his head off. What *more* would you like me to do? And what happened last night?'

'Nothing. Absolutely nothing!' said

Peter, dressing hurriedly. 'I mean, we didn't get Elizabeth – she got into the house, took what she wanted, and got out again – and disappeared. And although there were seven people altogether in the garden, watching, nobody saw her. So you see – nothing happened. ALL RIGHT, MOTHER! I'M JUST COMING.'

He tore downstairs with his mother still calling him, ate his breakfast standing up, and then cycled to school at top speed. He yelled to Janet as he left her at the corner.

'Meeting tonight at five-thirty. Tell Pam and Barbara!'

The meeting was not very thrilling. After such high hopes of something really exciting happening the night before, everyone felt flat. Pam made them all cross by saying that if *she* had hidden in the garden she would certainly have heard or seen Elizabeth creeping by.

'You must have fallen asleep,' she said.

'You really must. I mean – *seven* of you there! And nobody heard a thing! I bet you fell asleep.'

'Be quiet,' said Peter crossly. 'You don't know what you're talking about, Pam. Now don't start again. Be QUIET!'

'Well,' said Pam, obstinately, 'all I can say is that if Elizabeth *really* didn't get in or out, and it seems like that to me, or you'd have heard her – then she must be hiding in some secret place *inside* the house.'

'The police searched all over it,' said Peter. 'I did think of that bright idea myself – but I gave it up when the policeman hunted all through the cottage last night without finding Elizabeth. After all, it's only a small place – no cellars – no attics. We did hear *one* thing of interest, though. The brother who's in France is arriving in this country today. Maybe he'll have something to say that will be of help.'

'Well – why don't you go and see him,

then?' said Pam, who was in a very persistent mood that day. 'You could tell him what *you* know – about Tom the stable-boy seeing Elizabeth in Gorton, for instance.'

'H'm. That's the first sensible remark you've made, Pam,' said Peter. He turned to Jack. 'Will you come with me, Jack? I'd like to see the brother, I must say.'

'Wuff-wuff-wuff!' said Scamper, suddenly.

'*Now* what's the matter?' said Peter, whose late night had made him decidedly impatient that day. 'What's Scamper barking for? If it's Susie I'll have a few sharp words to say to her about playing that stupid trick on us with the suitcase!'

It *was* Susie. She stood grinning at the door when Peter opened it. 'Mint Sauce!' she said promptly. 'Let me in. I've some clues – great big ones. I know where Elizabeth is and what she's doing. I—'

'You do NOT!' yelled a furious Peter,

and called for Jack. 'Jack get her out of
here! Pam, Barbara, Janet – get hold of her
dress and pull, too. Come on! Get going!'

And for once in a way the cheeky Susie
was taken by surprise and found herself
being dragged to the gate, and not very
gently either!

'All right!' she yelled, kicking and hitting
out as vigorously as she could. 'I shan't tell
you my big clues. But you'll see I'm right!
And I know your password, see! Mint
sauce, Mint sauce, Mint sauce!'

She disappeared up the lane, and the
Seven went back to the shed, feeling better for the excitement. 'Now we shall
have to alter our password,' said Peter,
in disgust. 'How did Susie know it, Jack?
Have you been saying it in your sleep, or
something?'

'No,' said Jack, still angry. 'She must
have hidden somewhere near the shed
and heard us saying it. Bother Susie! You

don't think she really *does* know something, do you?'

'How can she?' said Peter. 'And why can't you keep her in order? If Janet behaved like that I'd give her a piece of my mind.'

'You would *not*,' said Janet, indignantly. 'You just try it!'

'Gosh – we really are crosspatches to-day!' said Barbara, surprised. 'The boys must be tired after their late night! Well – have we any plans?'

'Only that Jack and I will go and see Elizabeth's brother, if he's arrived at the grandmother's,' said Peter, calming down. 'He'll be sure to go there, because his sister is known to be somewhere near. Come on, Jack – I'm fed up with this meeting. Let's go!'

[16]

Unexpected news

Peter and Jack arrived at Bramble Cottage on their bicycles, and at once heard voices there. They put their cycles by the gate and looked over the hedge.

Three people were sitting in deck-chairs in the little garden, enjoying the warm evening sunshine. One was Miss Wardle – one was an old lady, obviously the grandmother – and one was a youth of about eighteen, looking very worried.

'He must be the brother,' said Peter. 'Good, he's arrived! Come on. We'll go up the front path, and if Miss Wardle sees us, she'll call us and we'll go over and talk.'

Miss Wardle did see them, and recognised them at once. 'Oh,' she said to the old lady beside her, 'those are the two nice boys who brought all that jumble. Come here, boys – I'm sure Mrs Sonning would like to thank you.'

Peter and Jack walked over. 'Good evening,' said Peter, politely. 'I do hope you have news of your granddaughter, Mrs Sonning.'

'No. We haven't,' said the old lady, and to Peter's alarm, a tear rolled down her cheek. 'This is my grandson, Charles, her brother. He's come over from France to see if he can help, because Elizabeth is very fond of him. If she knows he is here, she may come out of hiding.'

'We met a boy the other day who saw her in Gorton,' said Peter. 'She must have been on her way here then.'

'What!' said the boy Charles. 'Someone actually saw her in *Gorton*! But that's *not* on the way here. Who was this boy?'

'One of the stable-boys up at Warner's

Stables there,' said Peter, pointing up the hill. 'He said Elizabeth told him she was going to France to see you.'

'But she didn't know where I *was* in France,' said Charles. 'I've been travelling around all the time! Even the police only got in touch with me with great difficulty! I'm certain that Elizabeth wouldn't have been mad enough to try to find me when she didn't even know what part of France I was in!'

'Well,' said Peter, 'that's what *Tom* said she told him, and he couldn't very well have made it up, because he had never met her before!'

'I'll go and see him,' said Charles, and got up – but just then the telephone bell shrilled out, the noise coming clearly into the garden.

'Answer it, Charles, there's a dear,' said old Mrs Sonning, and the boy went indoors. Peter and Jack waited patiently for him, and were immensely surprised to see him come running out again at top speed, his eyes shining and his face aglow.

'Granny! It was Elizabeth's headmistress. She—'

'Oh – has the child gone back to school – or gone back to her aunt?' said the old lady.

'No! But all that upset about the stolen money is cleared up!' said Charles, taking his grandmother's hand. 'It *wasn't* Elizabeth who took it, of course. The girl who stole it got frightened when the papers kept reporting that Elizabeth hadn't been found, and she suddenly owned up.'

'Who *was* the girl?' said Miss Wardle, indignantly.

'I'm afraid it was the one supposed to be Elizabeth's best friend,' said Charles. 'Lucy Howell – she came here to stay with Elizabeth last year, Granny. She saw the cash-box in the desk and took it on the spur of the moment, without even opening it. She hid it somewhere, waiting for a chance to break it open. She didn't realise that there was about a hundred pounds in it, and she was horrified when the police were called in about it.'

'I should think so!' said Mrs Sonning. 'I never did like Lucy – a sly little thing I thought she was. I was sorry that she was Elizabeth's friend.'

'Well, apparently Lucy was annoyed with Elizabeth and very jealous of her just then, because Elizabeth was ahead of her in marks and doing better at games – and what did she do but take the cash-box and put it into Elizabeth's chest of drawers! When the boarders' trunks and chests were searched – Elizabeth is a weekly boarder as you know – the cash-box was found – still unopened! Elizabeth had gone home for the weekend to Aunt Rose's, and the police went there to question her.'

'Poor Elizabeth!' said Mrs Sonning. 'But didn't she deny taking the money?'

'Yes, of course – but she wasn't believed. Most unfortunately she had actually been in the classroom where the money had stupidly been left, doing some homework all by herself, and had been seen there. Aunt Rose was very upset – and poor Elizabeth felt there was nothing to do but run away! I expect she thought she might have to go to prison or something!'

'Poor child! But now she can come back with her name cleared!' said Mrs Sonning. 'What a dreadful thing to happen to someone like Elizabeth. She's as honest as can be.'

'Yes. But how are we going to let her know that everything is all right?' asked Miss Wardle. 'We don't even know where the child is!'

'No. That's true,' said Charles, worried. 'But we *must* find her! She took only enough money with her to pay her railway fare down here apparently – that's all she had. She wouldn't have enough to buy food or anything else. She's hiding somewhere, all alone worried and miserable – thinking that we're all ashamed of her!'

'Don't,' said old Mrs Sonning, and began to weep into her handkerchief. 'Such a dear, good child – always so kind. Charles, we must find her – we must!'

'Well – the first thing to do is for me to go up and see this stable-boy who met Elizabeth in Gorton,' said Charles, getting up. 'Will you take me up to him, you two boys?'

'Yes,' said Peter and Jack, who had been listening to the conversation with much interest. 'We'll take you now. We are so glad everything's cleared up!'

[17]

A *funny business altogether*

Peter, Jack, and Charles went to the gate at the bottom of the little garden, and up the hill to Warner's Stables, the two boys wheeling their bicycles. They liked Charles. He reminded them of someone, but they couldn't think who it was.

'Where's Tom?' Peter called to Harry, when they came to the stables. He was saddling a horse.

'Somewhere about,' he shouted back. 'Over there, I think.'

'You see if Tom is over there, and I'll go into the stables and see if he's there,' said Peter. Charles went with Jack, and Peter looked into the stables. At the far end he saw Tom, cleaning out one of the stalls.

'Hey, Tom!' called Peter. 'There's some-one wants to see you.'

'Who?' shouted back Tom.

'You remember meeting that girl Eliza-beth?' said Peter. 'Well, it's her brother, Charles. He's come over from France, he's so upset, and—'

He stopped, because Tom had suddenly flung down his rake, and had shot past him at top speed. He tore out of the door, and Peter stared in surprise. When Peter got to the stable door himself, there was no sign of Tom! He saw Jack and Charles coming towards him, and called to them.

'Did you see Tom? He tore out of here just now, goodness knows why!'

'We saw someone racing off,' said Jack. 'Bother! Just as we wanted him. Didn't you tell him someone wanted to see him?'

'Yes, of course. I don't know if he heard me or not, but he suddenly flung down his

fork and dashed off without a word!' said
Peter, puzzled.

Harry, the other stable-boy, came up
with the big stable-girl. 'Don't take any
notice of Tom,' he said. 'He's a bit odd!
Isn't he, Kate?'

The stable-girl nodded. 'Hasn't got much
to say for himself,' she said. 'Funny boy – a
bit potty, *I* think!'

'But where did he go?' said Peter. 'Do
you know where he lives? We could go
to his home, and then our friend here
could ask him a few things he wants to
know.'

Neither Harry nor the girl knew where
Tom lived, so Jack and Peter gave it up.
'Sorry,' they said to Charles and Peter
added: 'We could come here again tomorrow if you like. Not that Tom can really tell
you anything of importance. He may even
have made it all up about meeting Elizabeth. He may have read about her in the

papers, and just invented the whole meeting! He really *is* a bit odd, I think.'

'Well – thank you,' said Charles, who looked worried again. 'I'll go back. My poor old granny won't be herself again till we find Elizabeth. My parents haven't been told yet, but they'll have to be rung tomorrow, and asked to come home. Dad's out in China on a most important job, and we didn't want to worry him at first. Apparently the police thought they would soon find my sister.'

'Yes – with no money – and wearing her school clothes it *ought* to have been easy to spot her,' said Jack. 'Well – goodbye – and good luck!'

The boys rode off down the hill. 'I'm really glad Elizabeth didn't steal that money after all,' said Peter. 'Though we've never met her, I thought it was rather strange that anyone said to be so honest and straightforward should have done such a thing. And now I've seen that old granny, and her nice brother Charles – he *is* nice, isn't he, Jack? – I see even more clearly that Elizabeth couldn't have been a thief.'

'It's a funny business altogether,' said Jack. 'And it's not cleared up yet, Peter – not till Elizabeth's found. Remember, *she* doesn't know that the real thief has owned up!'

'I know,' said Peter. 'Well – we'll have another Secret Seven meeting tomorrow night, the same time as today, Jack. We'll tell the others at school tomorrow. We'll have to report this evening's happenings, and see if there's anything further we can do.'

'Right!' said Jack. 'See you tomorrow!' and with a jingling of bicycle bells the two parted, each thinking the same thing: what a pity Elizabeth doesn't know that her name is cleared!

Next evening the Secret Seven gathered in the meeting shed as usual, anxious to hear

what Jack and Peter had to say. They were
all very thrilled to hear about the brother
Charles – and the exciting telephone call
that had come while Jack and Peter were
there.

'What a pity that boy Tom didn't stop
and speak to Charles,' said Colin, puzzled.
'Do you suppose he made up that tale about
meeting Elizabeth, and was afraid of being
found out in his fairy-tale by Charles?'

'*I* tell you what!' said George, suddenly. 'I
believe he knows where Elizabeth is! That's
why he acts so strangely! That's why he ran
off like that – to warn her that her brother
was there!'

'You may be right, George,' said Peter,
considering the matter. 'Yes – perhaps he
does know where she is! Well – all the more
reason why we should go up tomorrow and
see him! We'll ask him straight out if he
knows where the girl is – and watch his face.
He's sure to give himself away if he *does*

know where she is – even if he swears he doesn't!'

'We'll tell Charles to come too,' said Jack. 'If *he* thinks Tom knows his sister's hiding-place, I've no doubt he'll be able to make him tell it!'

'Right,' said Peter. 'Well – tomorrow may be exciting. We'll just see!'

[18]

Peter goes mad

The next evening the Seven took their bicycles and went riding to Warner's Stables once more, leaving a message at Bramble Cottage for Charles to follow, if he wished. He was out when they called.

Harry and the stable-girl were carting straw about the yard, but Tom was nowhere to be seen.

'He asked if he could work down in the fields today,' said Harry. 'Not in the stables. You could bike down to them, if you want him. He's a bit touchy today, is old Tom!'

'If someone called Charles comes along, tell him where we are,' said Peter. 'That's the boy who was with us yesterday.'

They rode down to the fields, and saw

Tom in the distance exercising ponies round the meadow. They shouted to him and waved.

He stopped and looked hard at them all. Then he waved back and came cantering over.

'Sorry I'm busy,' he said. 'Is there anything you want?'

'Yes!' said Peter, putting his bicycle by the gate and climbing over the top bar. 'Tom – I want to ask you a question. Do you know where Elizabeth Sonning is hiding? *Do* you?'

A frightened look came into Tom's face. 'Why should I know that?' he said. 'Don't be crazy!' And with that he kicked his heels against the pony's side and galloped off!

'He does know! He does!' said Jack. 'And he won't tell.' He turned to Peter and looked suddenly astonished. 'Why, Peter – what on earth's the matter? Why are you looking like that?'

Peter did indeed look peculiar – astonished – bewildered – as if someone had knocked him on the head. Jack shook him, quite scared.

'Peter! What is it?'

'Gosh – of *course* he knows where Elizabeth is!' said Peter. 'Nobody in the world knows better where Elizabeth hides out! Nobody!'

'Peter!' cried everyone, wondering if he had suddenly gone mad. What in the world did he mean?

He didn't answer, but did something very surprising. He lifted his bicycle over the gate into the field, mounted it and rode over the grass after Tom, who was still cantering along, on the pony.

The Seven stared open-mouthed. No doubt about it – Peter had gone off his head! Now he was shouting at the top of his voice.

'Come here, you idiot! Everything's all

right! Elizabeth! COME HERE! I've got good news for you! Elizabeth! ELIZABETH!'

'Mad,' said Jack, looking quite scared. They all stood and watched, really amazed.

Now Peter was cycling quite near to Tom and his rather frightened pony, and he was still shouting.

'Everything's all right, I tell you! Lucy Howell confessed *she* took the money! Everyone knows it wasn't you! WILL you stop, you idiot, and listen to me?'

And at last the pony stopped, and the rider allowed Peter to cycle up and jump off by its side. The six by the gate poured into the field to hear what was happening.

Peter was out of breath, but he still talked. 'You're Elizabeth! I know you are! I *knew* your brother reminded me of someone – and I suddenly saw the likeness just now at the gate! Elizabeth, it's all right. Your name's cleared. And look – there's your brother at the gate. Come now – you *are* Elizabeth, aren't you?'

Tears began to fall down the girl's face. 'Yes – I *am* Elizabeth Sonning! Oh, is it true that Lucy said she took the money? I thought she had – but I wasn't sure. Nobody will think me a thief any more?'

'Nobody,' said Peter. 'Well, you're a brave kid, aren't you – getting a job as a stable-boy, and working hard like this! Where did you hide at night? How—?'

'Oh – there's Charles!' cried Elizabeth, suddenly, though the Seven still couldn't help thinking of her as Tom, of course! The girl galloped her pony over to Charles, shouting to him: 'Charles! Charles! Oh, I'm so glad to see you!'

She almost fell off her pony into his arms, and the two hugged one another tightly. The Seven went over to them, feeling excited and pleased. What a surprising ending to the problem they had been puzzling over so long!

'Well, you monkey!' said Charles, who suddenly looked much younger. 'What have you got to say for yourself? Bringing me over from France like this – having everyone hunting for you? Where have you been hiding? How did you get in and out of Granny's house? Why—?'

'Oh, Charles – I'll answer all your questions!' said Elizabeth, half-crying and half-laughing. 'But let's go to Granny's, do let's. I do want to hug her, I do want to tell her everything's all right!'

'Come on, then,' said Charles, putting his arm round his sister. He turned to the Seven. 'You kids can come too,' he said. 'We've a lot to thank you for – and I'm longing to know how you spotted that this dirty, untidy, smelly stable-boy was no other than my naughty little sister Elizabeth.'

[18]

A jolly good finish

They all went out of the field, and took the path that led down to Bramble Cottage. The Seven were very thrilled to be in at the finish. To their great disgust they met Susie on her bicycle, riding along with a friend.

'Hallo!' she called cheekily. 'Solved your silly mystery yet?'

'Yes!' said Jack. 'And that boy Tom was Elizabeth – dressed up like a stable-boy. *You'd* never have thought of that in a hundred years!'

'Oh, but I knew it!' said the aggravating Susie. 'Shan't tell you how! But I knew it!' And away she went, waving her cheeky hand at them.

'She's a terrible fibber,' said Janet. 'I

suppose she *couldn't* have guessed, could she, Jack?'

'I wouldn't put it past her,' said Jack, with a groan. 'Anyway, she'll keep on and on saying she knew. *Why* did I tell her just now?'

'Goodness knows,' said Peter. 'You'd better safety-pin your mouth, Jack! Well – here we are at the cottage. Won't the old granny be pleased?'

She was! She hugged the brown-faced, short-haired girl and kissed her, happy tears streaming down her face.

Miss Wardle rushed indoors and brought out biscuits and lemonade for everyone. Scamper, who was there as usual, of course, was delighted to have two fine biscuits presented to him.

'Elizabeth! Now where did you hide? And are those *my* riding-breeches?' asked Charles, pulling at them. 'Where did you get them?'

'From your chest of drawers here,' said Elizabeth. 'I knew nobody would miss them. They're rather big for me, though. And I've made them very dirty! I hid in the hayloft at the stables each night, with just a rug to cover me. I was quite warm and cosy.'

'So you *did* take that rug!' said Miss Wardle. 'I thought so! And all that food too, I suppose?'

'Yes. You see, I'd no money left after paying my fare down here,' said Elizabeth. 'At least, I had five pence, that's all. So I had to get a job – but you're only paid once a week, so I had to have food till my wages were due – I couldn't go without eating!'

'You poor child!' said Miss Wardle. 'Bless you, I knew you were innocent, I knew you weren't a thief! Yes, and I cooked special tarts and pies for you, my little dear, and left them out, hoping you'd come and take them.'

'Oh – thank you!' said Elizabeth. 'I did wonder why there was such a *lot* of food in the larder – and food I especially liked!'

'Why did you tell us that you had met – well, met *yourself* in Gorton, and all that?' asked Peter, puzzled.

'Only to put you off the scent,' said Elizabeth. 'I thought if people imagined I was off to France to find Charles, they wouldn't guess I was hiding near Granny's. I had to come near Granny's because of getting food, you see – and, anyway, I wanted to *feel* I was near somebody belonging to me, I was so miserable.'

'How did you get into the house, Elizabeth?' said Miss Wardle, and Charles chimed in with:

'Yes – how did you?'

And Peter added, 'Why, the other night we all watched here in the garden – but, how very funny, you were here too, Elizabeth, pretending to watch for yourself – you were Tom, up that tree! *Were* you up the tree?'

Elizabeth laughed. 'Yes, of course. That tree has a branch that goes to the bathroom window – and I know how to open the window from the outside and slip in – I'll show you, it's quite easy if you have a pocket-knife. But I'm getting too large to squeeze through it now, really! It really made me laugh to think of everyone watching and waiting – and there was I, up the tree, waiting to slip through the window. I got a lovely lot of food that night – did you see my torch shining in the downstairs rooms? And I was just sliding down the tree again when I heard the police knocking on the front door.'

'And you told us not to tell the police you were there – because you knew your pockets were full of food!' said Peter, with a chuckle. 'Yes, I think your brother's right. You really are a monkey.'

'But I was a very, very good stable-boy,' said Elizabeth, earnestly. 'Granny, Mr Warner said he was very pleased with me, and he even promised me a rise in wages if I went on working so hard! Can I go on being a stable-boy? It's nicer than being at school.'

'Certainly not!' said her grandmother, smiling. 'You'll go back to school and be welcomed there by everyone – and you'll work hard and be top of the exams, although you've missed a week and a half!'

'But what *I* want to know is – how did *you*, Peter, realise so suddenly that Tom the stable-boy was Elizabeth?' asked Charles.

'Well – I suddenly saw the likeness between you,' said Peter. 'And then somehow the bits of the jigsaw all fell into place, if you know what I mean! And I was so afraid that Elizabeth would run off again when she saw you, as she did when she heard you were at the stables yesterday, that I just felt I had to cycle at top speed after her pony and yell at her!'

'I was never so surprised in my life as when you came at me and my pony at sixty miles an hour on your bike, yelling at the top of your voice,' said Elizabeth. 'But I'm glad you did. Granny, I'm coming here for the holidays, aren't I? Can I have these children to play sometimes?'

'Of course!' said her grandmother. 'I shall always be glad to see them. There's only one thing I'm sad about Elizabeth – your hair! *What* a pity you hacked it short like that. It was so soft and pretty!'

'I had to, Granny,' said Elizabeth. 'I did it with your nail scissors when I came one night to take Charles' riding-breeches to wear – and I took his jersey too, though it's so dirty now I don't expect he recognises it! Oh, Granny – I'm so very happy. You can't *think* how different I feel!'

'We'd better go,' said Peter to the others,

in a low voice. 'Let's leave them all to be happy together. Come on, say goodbye.'

They said goodbye, and Scamper gravely shook paws as well. Then away they went on their bicycles, Scamper running beside them.

'What a wonderful finish!' said Jack. 'Who would have thought it would end like that? I feel rather happy myself! When's the next meeting, Peter?'

'Tomorrow – and we'll have a celebration to mark our success!' said Peter. 'Everyone must bring some food or drink. And we'll have to think of a new password, of course. What shall it be?'

'Stable-boy!' said Jack at once.

Well, it's quite a good one – but I mustn't tell you if it's the *right* one. Knock on the door of the shed, say 'Stable-boy!' and see if the Secret Seven let you in!